ALIEN'S MERCY

OUTLAW PLANET MATES

LESLIE CHASE

THE WORLD OF OUTLAW PLANET
MATES

Reazus Prime is a hard planet. Once a prison, it was abandoned once the mines dried up and the Overlords could no longer turn a profit off the prisoners. Now it's a haven for outlaws, pirates, and anyone holding a grudge against authority.

It's isolated, alone, and the only ships coming are the worst sort. One such ship carrying a cargo of abducted human women, explodes in orbit. A lucky few were ejected in pods, only to crash on the outlaw planet.

Now the race is on to find and claim the human females.

MERCY

This wasn't the first time I'd woken up and not known where I was, but I'd never woken up in a coffin before. At least that's what it felt like; a space just big enough to fit me and no more, and even more uncomfortable than I'd have expected. *Perhaps it's because I'm face down,* I thought through the fog clouding my brain. That much at least made sense. I dimly remembered drinking and loud music.

Parts of the night before came back as I lay there. I'd been at Emily's bachelorette party, so of course I'd drunk more than was sensible. I was happy for Emily, yes, and wanted to celebrate, but when I was the last singleton in our group of friends, it was easy to get melancholy. Drowning that out with alcohol wasn't a great idea, but apparently it was the one I'd picked.

Which meant all kinds of wild shenanigans were on the table. Ending the night sleeping it off in a coffin wasn't the most ridiculous thing I could imagine. Emily's Maid of Honor, Megan, loved the goth scene even more than Emily did.

Flashes of memory floated past, blurs of color and sound. Somewhere, Megan found a stripper Dracula. Drinks, lots of drinks. Four of us staggering around the block arm in arm, God, what were we singing? The drink hadn't left me with a headache, but the memory might.

Were we even singing the same song? Other flashes of memory surfacing. Emily's rambling explanation of why she loved Mark so much. 'Dracula' dressed in nothing but a thong, a cape, and novelty fangs— Emily laughing so hard she fell off her chair. The world dissolving into a greenish haze, replaced by a strange, off-white room. Meeting Megan's cute, sweet girlfriend who drank us all under the table.

Wait. Go back a step.

I'd gone out for some air, and then… that couldn't be right. It just couldn't. I remembered green beam of light catching me, everything felt wrong, like I was falling upward, the green getting brighter and brighter before vanishing in an instant. Instead of standing on a footpath, I was in a huge off-white room full of people. Glossy black cylinders rose from the floor, suspiciously person-sized, most with hatches open.

That has to be a hallucination. Obviously. Maybe someone spiked my drink with acid? I don't think any of Emily's friends are the kind of asshole to do that, but you never know. The memory was clear, though, clearer than any of the other memories of the night past the first couple of shots.

The big room had been full of two kinds of people—other women, in various states of confusion and dressed in everything from what looked like arctic survival gear to just-stepped-out-of-the-shower naked and dripping. Some shouted, some cried, some tried to make themselves understood. Dozens of languages piled on top of each other, the cacophony pounding into my already-sore head.

Then there were the little green men. Yes, I know how that sounds, but they were small, they were green, and from the way they shoved the girls around, I assumed they were men. I stumbled forward as one pushed me with surprising strength, barking an order at me in a language I didn't understand. When I tried to tell him that, he hissed something and pressed a gadget to my arm. It stung for a moment, then the meaningless babble turned into words.

"Into the pod, animal, don't hold us up," my captor repeated, still speaking the same language… but somehow, I knew what the words meant now. Between the shock, the drink, and the sudden realization that this was really happening, I froze. The alien had no patience for that.

"You animals are so stupid, can't even follow simple orders." A hard shove sent me staggering back into one of the person-sized cylinders, and the hatch swung shut with a bang.

Then nothing until now. "Okay, that's one hell of a dream," I said aloud, just for the comfort of hearing the words. In the small space, they sounded flat, dead, and not at all reassuring. I squirmed, feeling out the shape of my confinement as the fog lifted from my thoughts.

Not a coffin. It was circular, with padding above me and a cold, hard surface below. Hanging onto the hope that this was somehow an example of Megan's dark humor, I tried to find a latch, a switch, anything.

I don't know what I did. I'm not even sure I found anything. Either I brushed a control, or something else unlocked the hatch, but without warning the hatch opened and I fell through into cold, bracing air full of the smell of the sea. My desperate flailing hands caught the edge of the hatch on the left, and a tree branch on my right, and my fall jerked to a stop.

Below me, far below me, waves crashed onto jagged rocks. I swallowed and tried not to look down. It wasn't easy to tear my eyes away, but there wasn't any point in staring at the death that waited for me to slip. Instead, I looked around for a way up.

Somehow, the black cylinder had gotten itself wedged between a cliff face and the tree that grew from it. A tree like nothing I'd seen before, leaves black as the coffee I craved, bark white, shiny, and prickly. It stung my hand, but not badly enough to make me risk letting go.

The cliff stretched off into the distance in both directions, steep and forbidding. I swore under my breath but put off thinking about the climb. It could wait until I wasn't dangling above a deadly fall. The odd bark made it hard for my scrabbling feet to find any purchase, and I thanked God I'd worn my boots rather than the pumps I might have chosen. They weren't the most sensible footwear in the world, but at least they stayed on and protected my feet from the prickly tree.

My right foot got nowhere, but I wedged my left between into a hole in the tree's trunk and rested my weight on it. Just in time, too—my left hand slipped, and if I hadn't braced myself against the tree, I'd have fallen to the wave-pummeled rocks. Okay, time to reassess. Even getting to the cliff was beyond me, let alone climbing it.

Time for plan Z, then. I hate plan Z.

"Help!" My voice sounded thin and reedy to me, and I winced at the note of desperation in it. I took a deep breath, gathered my energy, and shouted again.

My grip on the tree started slipping as I yelled, my palm slick with sweat. If no one heard me soon, I'd fall. If I fell, I'd better hope for a quick death. My voice trembling, I shouted over and over, hoping against the odds that someone would find me.

Focused on the dual tasks of crying for help and clinging to the tree, I didn't notice anyone approaching until someone shouted down to me. I nearly jumped out of my skin, and worse, out of the tree.

Once I'd stabilized my grip, I looked up to see three people peering over the cliff top. Blinking, I looked again. Either I was hallucinating, or they weren't human.

Two were identical, or near as could be. Green-skinned, with broad beaks for mouths and dark hair, they had rippling muscles and wore silver chains around their necks. Whatever they were, they stared at me with an interest that I could only call predatory. Narrow eyes looked down at me, assessing me as though I was an asset, a thing. I knew that look too well, and it was as obvious on an alien face as on a human's.

The third was different. Strikingly different. Deep purple skin was marked with gold patterns matching the color of his hair, and a rugged face etched with lines of experience gazed down. His eyes didn't have the appraising look the others did. Instead, he watched me with an aching sadness like I'd never seen before. He stood a head taller than the others, broad-shouldered and muscular.

Either I was still dreaming, or I wasn't on Earth anymore.

2

VARDOK

Do not ask me what day it was. Every day on that hell-hole planet was much the same—wake before dawn, eat whatever I could put together, and wait for my captors to begin their day. They slept late and gorged themselves on actual food, not the over-processed 'food' they fed their slaves.

Once they were ready, I'd accompany them on their rounds and do their dirty work for them. The Akkark brothers were lazy, which would be a failing in most people, but for bastards like these, it was a virtue. They were tough, mean, and hardy, but they'd spend their time on enjoying themselves when they should have been working, and that meant less harm for the people who lived on their circuit.

Less, but still too much. We were on our way back to Railhead with twenty new slaves they'd gathered on this round of their circuit, grabbing anyone who looked hardy enough to work the mines. The excuse was always the same—unpaid debts. No one mentioned the fact that those debts were unpayable by design and no farm on the island the Blood Talons controlled could be debt free. Everyone knew it was just an excuse and pointing it out only invited retribution.

Trudging through the rough landscape was no one's idea of fun, least of all those twenty unfortunates chained together by the necks. I didn't blame them for the glares they shot me. To them, I was just another oppressor. They had no way of knowing that I was as much a slave as they were, though the chains were on my soul rather than my body.

If I could have snapped the Akkark brothers' necks and freed the captives, I would. And if I could fly by flapping my arms, I'd be off this planet by now. There's little choice in a Roccarian warrior's life, and less for me than most.

"Hold up," Gor Akkark said, and the line of dejected slaves stopped without complaint. Chained one to the other, they looked glad for the chance to rest. Twenty males from six different species, walking in time was tough for a group like this, and the Akkarks cared no more about that than they did anything else outside of food and sex.

Kall Akkark wasn't so sanguine about a delay. "What is it now, Gor? I want to reach Railhead before sundown, and we're behind schedule."

Gor waved his brother to silence, looking off to the left. There wasn't much to see. Rough grassland, muddy from recent rain, surrounded us. Poisoned ground, unsafe to farm like most of this cursed island. Perhaps a hundred paces further on, the land came to an abrupt end at a cliff, and below it the sea.

The Akkarks kept a careful distance from the cliff, as they had since five years ago when a group of new slaves had leaped to their deaths rather than go to the korran ore mines. Probably the right choice, I had to acknowledge.

A cry for help, barely audible over the crash of waves, rose over the cliff and interrupted my thoughts and I sighed. No rescue waited for them, their shouts heard only by the slaver scum.

And me, I thought, though with every passing year, it got harder to count myself separate from the Blood Talons gang I had no choice but to serve.

The Akkarks ambled toward the cliff edge, gesturing for me to follow. We left the slaves behind, and I hoped they'd take the chance to get some rest —trying to escape would be the worst kind of foolishness.

All thought of them vanished when I reached the brothers and looked down. Whoever had crashed here had the wildest luck imaginable for their stasis pod to get stuck like that. Trapped between the rocks and the only tree in the area, the slightest change in angle would have made all the difference. A little higher, and the pod would have hit the grassland safely. Lower, and the rocks or the sea would have taken it and its occupant.

But it struck just right to trap them in the tree. Were they lucky or unlucky? I couldn't tell.

"There, look," Kall said, pointing down under the pod. "It's loose and trying to climb. Ten zek says it falls."

His brother rumbled disgust at that bet. "Mother should have eaten you as a hatchling, idiot. That's a human female, and she's worth more than the rest of those slaves put together."

"I know what it is." Kall clacked his beak shut, annoyed. "Doesn't mean we can't bet on it falling. You want in or not?"

While the two bickered, I moved around to see under the pod and stopped in my tracks.

I'd never seen a human before, female or no. If I'd seen anything like her, I'd remember. The woman hanging below the pod was beautiful, even at this distance. Her black clothing, as impractical as it was fetching, clung to her curves and did nothing to conceal them. Bright red hair whipped around her face in the wind, and green eyes stared back at me. One hand clung to the tree and she braced a foot against a hole in its trunk. The other scrabbled in vain for a handhold. In seconds, Kall would win his bet.

The thought of such a beauty falling to a watery death was like a dagger to my heart, but that was the inevitable conclusion of her struggle. And it might be a mercy compared to the fate that awaited her if she made it up the cliff.

Acting without orders would mean punishment. My enhancements, bound to the Akkarks, would see rebellion and turn my nerves against me. Even thinking about it made my skin burn. I didn't care. I would not watch the human die, no matter how much pain it caused me.

I felt the pulse of the enhancements laced through my muscles as I prepared to jump. Their extra power sent me soaring on a leap to the branches of the tree, landing with careful precision to avoid shaking the human loose. Wasted effort—she let out a shriek as I landed beside her and her flinch was enough to dislodge her from her precarious perch. Eyes as green as emeralds went wide, and the human dropped.

My hand closed on her arm almost before I'd thought of it, and it was an effort to keep my speed and strength under control so I didn't tear it off at the shoulder. For a long moment, we were still, her eyes meeting mine. My right hand held her at the elbow, my left clinging to a branch for balance.

A good thing too. When my hand closed on her arm, the contact was electric. Like a lightning bolt striking up from my fingers to my hearts, if the lightning bolt were made of joy. Every one of my senses kicked into overdrive, and my very soul lit up.

Her skin, delightfully soft in my hand, warm and firm. The sight of her, my eyes catching the widening of her pupils, the blush appearing on her cheeks and spreading down her neck. I heard her gasp, a tiny sound that mixed fear with shock and something more.

The human's scent filled my mind, complex and beautiful. Fear was there, yes, and alcohol, but also smoke and dance and laughter. Many years had passed since I'd encountered anything like it.

And beneath all those scents, there was her. I breathed deep, savoring it. The wonderful smell I hadn't known I needed, and now would never forget. She smelled of hope.

"Don't just hold her there, idiot, bring her up!" Kall's voice snapped me out of the experience, but I was in no hurry to obey his command. And curiously, my enhancements didn't respond by punishing me. The faintest buzz of pain flickered along them, a mere annoyance easily washed aside by the joy filling me.

Could I ignore the brothers' commands? I didn't want to hand the human over to those monsters, but did I have another option other than waiting for them to move on? I knew the Akkarks, and spite alone would have them wait there until we died or the stars burned out, whichever came first.

This is not my decision alone, I thought, straightening and pulling the human up to look her in the eyes. Between the wind and distance, the Akkarks wouldn't overhear us so long as we kept our voices low. "Those men are slavers. If I take you back to them, they will seek to sell you."

"Fuck my life," she said, an exhausted oath as she

slumped in my grip. A moment passed before she continued. "Um, whatever they have in mind, they're still right, aren't they? Not about the 'idiot' part! I'd just rather be standing on solid ground than abandoned here hanging onto a tree."

"I would never let you go."

Her pale skin glowed as blood rushed to her face, and I tried not to assume it meant the same in her species as in mine. On a fellow Roccarian, such a flush would have implied powerful emotions, particularly attraction. On a human, who knew?

"Fine, you'd hold me here until we starve to death," she said. "That's a *fantastic* plan."

"We would not starve. Lack of fresh water will kill us first."

The look she gave me made it clear that wasn't a comfort to her, but I did not want to lie. The electric connection between us made deceit unthinkable.

Something to ponder later, when I had time and privacy. Right now, the Akkark brothers were looking down at us, and the human agreed with them about the best course of action. And she was right, of course. I could not stay here forever, perched in a tree and waiting for death to find us. With great care, I lifted her over my shoulder, feeling her warmth through the thin layer of cloth she wore.

"Hold on tight," I said, and she obeyed without delay. When her arms took hold of me, I nearly lost my footing at the wave of delight her touch sent through me. It took an effort to push it aside and focus on my task, but there was no time to think about it now. As soon as she was secure, I leaped.

3

MERCY

I didn't scream as the alien giant launched himself into the air, but it wasn't for lack of trying. Slung over his shoulder, the power of his jump knocked the air out of my lungs before I had a chance. Behind us, the tree shook as we abandoned it, dislodging the cylinder I'd arrived in and sending it tumbling end over end to smash into the rocks below.

That could have been me. I tried not to stare in horror and hung onto my rescuer's harness for dear life.

The ride was surprisingly smooth, the alien hitting the cliff face and pulling himself up it in a single deft motion. I wouldn't call it comfortable, but it was, at least, short.

"Took you long enough." That had to be one of the beak-faced aliens, a nasty sneer in his voice. Unlike my captor, these aliens didn't impress me. They looked like turtles that had swallowed gangsters, leathery shells covering their bodies, powerful arms covered in crude tattoos. Cold red eyes looked at me over their beaks, the familiar unpleasant gaze of a man trying to picture me naked. Nothing about the pair gave me any reason to like or trust them.

I hoped my captor would stand up to them, but he disappointed me by staying silent. He hadn't let go of my arm yet, and there was a part of me that wanted to pull free of his grasp. That, I decided, was the stupid part of me.

Alien he might be, but I'd seen sympathy in his eyes. He'd rescued me, and I was sure he'd done it to save my life rather than to present me to his... employers? Owners? Whatever the turtle-men were to him.

So, how quickly does Stockholm Syndrome take to set in?

"You. Human." The turtle's voice stopped me from having to think about that. "How did you come to this planet? Is anyone after you? We'll keep you safe, don't worry. Trust the Akkark brothers."

Trust you about as far as I can throw you, sure. I

knew better than to say that aloud, though. Better to stay on their good side, if they had one. "I don't know, sorry. Everything's a blur. I-I think aliens abducted me. The next thing I knew, I woke up stranded on that cliff. Can you—"

The other turtle interrupted before I could try asking for a lift to wherever one got a spaceship to Earth from here. "A fresh-caught human? Untouched, unbred? We'll be rich, brother. So rich!"

"Quiet, Kall. Let me think about this."

Unbred? The word had implications I didn't like. I almost blurted out a question but bit it back. They weren't likely to tell me anything I could trust, but if they talked among themselves, I might overhear something useful.

"What's to think about, Gor? We've got our quota of workers and now this treasure falls into our hands. The Universe blesses us, we cannot refuse it."

"Shut up about the Universe, Kall. You don't want to attract its attention, not when we're in the middle of moving the slaves."

"They aren't slaves, they're indentures. If they paid their taxes, they'd be sitting at home now."

The other alien, Gor, rolled his eyes at that but didn't argue. I wasn't sure which I preferred—Gor's honest evil or Kall's hypocritical protestations of innocence. Neither of them changed anything for me.

They bickered, and I let my eyes drift away, wondering if I should simply make a run for it. One look at the landscape was enough to put me off that idea. To my left was the cliff I'd just come from. Nothing useful there. In every other direction, sickly grassland stretched to the horizon promised me nowhere to hide. I'd be easy to follow through those strange, pink and purple grasses, and while I could have chosen worse footwear, my boots weren't made for running. Nor was my dress. Nor, to be honest, was I.

The more I looked, the more forbidding and alien the terrain was. Even the sunlight was strange, and it took me a moment to realize that was because there were two suns in the sky.

Blood drained from my face and I felt weak at the knees, the world fading. Biting the inside of my mouth, I struggled to stay awake and on my feet despite my body's attempt to faint. Any hope I'd hung onto that I was still on Earth vanished, and with it the idea of running away.

Even if I escaped, where would I go? I had to stay with them until I got my bearings. Looking at the slaves, linked by thick chains and slumped on the ground, I didn't like that prospect either, but it was the only choice I saw.

As if on cue, Kall spoke. "Get her chained and we'll be off. We're wasting daylight."

My savior and captor's hand tightened on my arm, but he didn't move. His grip wasn't painful, it felt more supportive than anything else.

The muscles around Kall's beak tightened into hard lines. "You heard me, Vardok. Get her in chains."

"No," he said. A moment of shocked silence followed before he spoke again, taking a more moderate tone. "You want to put your prize possession in with that rabble? If anything happens to her there, you can't say I didn't warn you."

"None of them would dare," Kall protested. "They know what will happen if they damage her."

"They have little enough to live for. Ruining your day might be enough of a temptation."

Looking at the chained line of aliens, I swallowed. Vardok wasn't kidding—the anger in their eyes should have burned a hole through all of us. Give them a chance to hurt the slavers and someone would take it, even if it meant their own lives. I couldn't blame them, really, but that didn't mean I wanted to be the vehicle for their revenge.

I had no idea why I was so valuable to these asshole slavers, but it painted a target on me. Just my fucking luck.

The turtle-men looked at each other, then back at Vardok, giving him an unhappy nod. "Okay, but it's on you. If anything happens to her, you're the one who'll suffer for it."

"Nothing will happen to her," Vardok said, squeezing my arm. It felt reassuring, like he was making a promise to protect *me*, rather than protecting their investment. Which was a stupid thing to let myself believe, but I had to hang onto something.

The turtle-men glared, clacking their beaks and narrowing their eyes. But they said nothing, just turned and shouted at the chained slaves, roughly shoving them forward. Vardok followed, bringing me with him.

MARCHING in my party outfit was even less pleasant than I'd imagined it would be. The unfamiliar sun shone hot overhead, its harsh light a constant reminder that I wasn't on Earth anymore. I wished I had sunscreen. I was showing too much skin and adding the sting of sunburn to this day would be just perfect.

Beside me walked the towering block of muscle who'd rescued me, only to hand me over to these slavers. I couldn't help glancing sideways at him, and each time, my heart flip-flopped at his perfect body. He moved with the precise grace of a cat, always alert, totally controlled. And his leather pants were tight enough that I wondered if he might tear them by flexing his thighs. That thought gave me something to look forward to.

The golden markings on his skin shifted and changed as I watched, pulsing and flowing. Not just tattoos, then. We walked in silence for what felt like hours before the tension got to me, and I spoke.

"Thanks for saving me." Start with something positive, always a good strategy. But it didn't work on Vardok the way I'd hoped.

He laughed, a single cold and hard sound. "You should wait before you thank me. Soon enough you might wish we hadn't found you."

"Hey, whatever comes next, at least there's a next. I've got more chance of getting through that than surviving a fall onto those rocks."

"Ah. You're an optimist." Vardok made that word sound like a curse, or a mental illness. My lips tightened I shot him my best glare.

"I'm alive, and where there's life, there's hope. Perhaps the horse can learn to sing."

This time his laugh held some humor, but he shook his head. "I do not know what a horse is, but I know better. Still, I will do what I can to protect you, as long as I can."

He still hadn't let go of my arm, and as he spoke, a wave of warmth, of trust, flooded me from where our skins touched. It wasn't enough to make me back down, though. Vardok thought he 'knew better' but I'd show him that there's always hope to find if you look.

That wouldn't come from arguing with him, though. You couldn't argue someone into being hopeful, you had to give them a reason to hope instead. And I knew too little of this crazy world to do that.

So let's fix that and find out what the fuck's going on. "You've already saved my life once, and I haven't even introduced myself. Hi, I'm Mercedes Lang. My friends call me Mercy, and anyone who saves my life is my friend."

Vardok gestured with his free hand, graceful and

too fast for me to follow, touching his chest, lips, and forehead. "My name is Vardok ca'Brusi Irbak, Son of the House of Irbak, Enhanced Soldier."

I must have looked blank, because he followed up with an explanation immediately. "Brusi is the name of my mother, I am a legitimate member of Irbak by blood descent, and they optimized my body for war."

Another gesture, running down the golden veins on his deep blue skin. They pulsed as my eyes followed his hand.

"So, how did you end up…" I trailed off, rather than insult his employers. Vardok's laugh had nothing to do with humor. It came from a place of rage and hate and frustration.

"It turns out my skill in combat doesn't matter much when the troop transport I'm on gets shot out from under me. I woke as a prisoner of the Empire that used to own this planet."

"So this is a prisoner of war camp?"

"No, Mercy," he said, rolling my name in his mouth as though tasting it. I tried to ignore the blush spreading across my face at the sound. "This was a prison *planet,* before the Empire abandoned it. This island was a high security area, a place for the most dangerous criminals. And since the Empire refused to call my homeworld's rebellion a war, they treated me as just another criminal to be worked to death in the mines."

I looked him up and down, taking in his perfectly defined muscles, his smooth, firm skin I wanted to run my hands over, powerful hands that I wanted on me… *Mercedes Angelica Lang, stop that.*

The sensible voice in my head couldn't stop me from thinking about it, but it pushed me to speak. "You don't *look* like you've been worked to death."

"Hah, no, I do not. We Roccarians are tough, and my enhancements let me survive where others perished. I'm not sure that was a good thing."

"None of that," I said, poking my finger into his chest. It was like prodding a block of granite. "If you'd died, you wouldn't have been here to save me."

I didn't mean for him to take that seriously, but instead of laughing or scowling, he gave me a solemn nod.

"Yes, that is true. You are right, Mercy, it was worth the years of suffering to be there to rescue you."

Those words might have sounded sarcastic coming from anyone else. From Vardok, I couldn't doubt his sincerity. He genuinely thought that years in the hellhole he described were worth it for the chance to save me.

I'd have kissed him if not for the fear of what the slavers would do.

"So, what, the turtle-men are the guards?" I asked, trying to be practical. Daydreaming about kissing an alien warrior would wait, I needed to understand where I was.

A smile twitched at Vardok's full lips. "No. They are a prison gang. When the Empire pulled out, the Blood Talons took over this island and the mines and started running it for themselves. The island's ore veins are almost exhausted, but there's still enough left to make it worth their while—as long as they don't have to pay their workers."

"Or pay for safety precautions?"

Vardok nodded. "The Blood Talons don't care what happens to the miners. They just care about output, so they can buy luxuries for themselves."

The more I heard about this planet, the less I liked it.

4

VARDOK

Speaking with Mercy was a strange experience. It had been many years since I'd had a someone to share my thoughts and feelings with, caught between two worlds as I was. The convicts didn't trust me because I was bound to the guards, and when the Empire withdrew, the Blood Talons. But the rulers, whether guards or up-jumped prison gang, had no interest in me as anything other than an extension of their will.

Mercy was different. Different in more ways than I could count, and it took an effort not to blurt out every thought I had. She made my hearts sing, and I wanted to compose poetry to her beauty. I swear, had the other slaves made a break for it, I wouldn't have noticed. My focus was on her alone.

"So why are you working for these Blood Talons?" she asked. "You don't sound like you want to."

I answered her questions without a thought or hesitation, giving voice to things I hadn't addressed in years. Telling her things I'd kept secret from everyone on this planet, that only a Roccarian would know.

"The Empire had many faults, but lack of technical skill was not one of them. Their scientists worked out how to hack my enhancements. Not enough to deactivate them, or even to take full control of them, but enough to change the priority system around. They used the safety systems to enslave me."

Mercy frowned, and I continued. "To make sure the enhanced soldiers didn't turn on our leaders, the Roccarian military made the enhancements punish us if we disobeyed. The Empire turned that around so I would obey the guards, and when they withdrew, the guard commander sold that access to the Blood Talons. He went home rich, the Akkarks got me to act as their enforcer, and everyone else on this island got screwed."

I reined in my emotions, hearing the bitter darkness in my voice. I'd been drowning in a sea of despair ever since the Empire subverted my enhancements, but for the first time in those long years, I felt a spark of something else deep in my soul. Something I barely recognized. Hope.

The temptation to crush it nearly overwhelmed me. If I had no expectations, I couldn't be disappointed. But Mercy's touch pushed back the darkness and made me feel alive again. As we continued our march in silence, I let myself consider why. It wasn't just the pleasure of a beautiful female's company; it was a greater and deeper feeling than that.

Imprisoned here with no way to escape, I'd given up on finding my mate, but now I allowed myself to hope. Perhaps fate had brought her to me after all— my senses screamed at me that she was the one, and I wanted to believe them so badly it hurt. I'd known her for less than half a day, but in that time she'd shown empathy, humor, and a mental fortitude beyond what anyone could expect.

A pity her physical fortitude didn't live up to it. We hadn't been walking long before she tired, and I winced. Her clothing didn't help, the heels on her boots made walking awkward and the tight skirt of her black dress didn't help. As fetching as the outfit was, its designer had paid little attention to practical matters.

Perhaps, I thought, *it would be better if she took some of it off.*

Even I didn't believe that was an altruistic suggestion on my part. Mercy's outfit seemed designed to tantalize me, to make me want to tear it from her and feast my eyes on the beauty beneath. Lace covered her upper arms, the low cut of the dress showed off her cleavage, and it clung to her curves just right. Despite that, the beauty of Mercy's body couldn't compare to her face. Achingly beautiful, her red hair a tumbling firefall framing a face that ought to be immortalized in art, though any sculptor who captured it would break his tools in despair of ever crafting anything so perfect again.

Green eyes looked up at me, wide and curious, frightened and trusting. I knew I couldn't trust myself to read her emotions—we'd barely met, and she was the first of her species I'd encountered—but somehow, I understood her.

While I'd have loved to learn about her, the pace the Akkark brothers set was punishing and Mercy had no strength to spare for conversation. Our captors might be decadent little shits, but they were hardy too, and when they set their mind to some-thing, they put the work in.

Mercy, ill-equipped for the journey, suffered even more than the others. As the sun dipped toward the horizon, she flagged and fell behind.

"You must keep up," I said, keeping my voice low. "The Akkarks have no patience for those who can't, and while you are too valuable to harm, they can find many ways to hurt you."

I heard the anger in my words, the rage at the very idea of Kall and Gor punishing this wonderful woman. My enhancements burned, not painfully but furiously, and the urge to kill rose in my heart. Again, no pain followed, and again, I put that mystery aside. The human needed help, and that took priority.

"Sorry," Mercy said, trying to walk faster. It lasted all of five steps. "I've walked further today than I have in years."

"Do not apologize. You have done nothing wrong, but that will not save you from them."

I looked ahead to where the brothers harangued the chained slaves. Neither had any attention to spare for us. Mercy was safe while they were distracted, but that wouldn't last forever.

"How can I help you?" I asked. Before she could

give the obvious answer, I continued. "No, carrying you won't work. I am supposed to be on guard, and the Akkarks will not accept me burdening myself. There are too many ambush predators out here."

A pleasing blush spread across her face as she hissed her reply. "I wouldn't ask you to carry me. I'm not a child!"

I raised an eyebrow and said nothing. Her blush deepened. We both know she would have asked had I not spoken first.

"Fine. In that case, you can distract me from how tired I am, how much my legs hurt, and how fucking ridiculous this fucking situation is."

"How shall I distract you?" I knew how I wanted to do it but dragging her off into the long grass and fucking her until she melted into a mewling puddle of pure pleasure wasn't a practical option. The way her eyes flashed made me suspect Mercy had the same idea. Fortunately, she had another idea, too.

"Tell me about your home? Something happier than this place."

So I did. As we walked, I told her of Roccar, of our double moons, and my home above the great tidal plains. How the twin tides would bring beautiful crystal wingfish to our farm each flood season, and how my sister had trained one to return to her every year. And Mercy hung on every word, forgetting her pain and fear.

It wasn't just Mercy who was distracted by my stories of home. I'd put them out of my mind long ago as too painful to remember and speaking of my family made my hearts ache. I barely noticed the shadows lengthening until the sun vanished behind the mountains and we still hadn't reached Railhead.

The air cooled fast as daylight fled, and my eyes shifted to night vision mode. The others weren't lucky enough to have the enhancements I did, and our group slowed to a crawl. No matter what threats the Akkarks hissed at their slaves, there was nothing anyone could do to speed them up—each time they tried, one would stumble or trip and bring the whole chained group to a stop.

They did their best to hurry, though. No one wanted to camp out in the toxic wilderness, prey for any predators that came along. The Blood Talons ruled this island with an iron fist, but outside the walls at night, the entire island was a deadly trap. The distant light of Railhead's walls gave us a target to aim for, and the path got smoother as we approached.

Nothing much had changed since the Empire left. The blocky, brutal architecture of the guard compound remained unchanged save for a crude crimson talon daubed on either side of the gate. Guards on the wall let us get far too close before they saw and challenged us, and I snorted in disgust at their lax attitude. Roccar would never have tolerated such poor discipline.

Gor Akkark called back, identifying us, and the great gates swung aside. Though I'd passed through the gateway thousands of times, I paused at the threshold. This time, the opening looked like the vast maw of some giant monster, ready to swallow Mercy whole as I led her through it.

5

———

MERCY

*E*ntering the forbidding compound, I wondered if perhaps I should have made a break for it after all. The place looked like a prison from some dystopian nightmare, hard edged-concrete and high walls. Though, if what Vardok told me was true, the prison was everything outside the walls.

Beyond the gates, we entered a central courtyard, overlooked by a monolithic building that loomed menacingly above us. Narrow windows, a heavy door, and mounted searchlights made it look like a fortress, which I supposed it was. Built into the wall, it dominated the compound, but smaller buildings ran along the inside of the walls as well. They looked newer, cruder, built of wood rather than stone. And they smelled. The whole courtyard stank of old sweat and fear and blood, and I shivered at the sight of dark stains on the paving.

A group of aliens waited to greet us. They came in many shapes and sizes, but they all had one thing in common—each wore the bloody claw symbol somewhere prominent. Even without that clue, I'd have spotted them as gang members from the fact that they had weapons. Most carried batons, but a few held heavy, odd-shaped guns. Lasers, I guessed, but how would I know?

One stood out from the group, a head taller than the others, covered in shaggy white fur. Four arms stretched out in greeting as the Akkarks approached, and a wide grin split his face, baring sharp, meat-tearing fangs.

"Kall, Gor, welcome," he said, voice booming to fill the courtyard. "You had me worried when you didn't show up by sundown. I was on the verge of sending out a search party."

"No need for that, Shadran," Gor said. "Just a minor delay, and anyway, we've got our own protection."

He clapped Vardok's arm and grinned. Both he and Shadran were full of shit. I'd seen enough macho posturing in my time to understand the subtext—

that over-enthusiastic friendliness could only mean they hated each other. So, of course, they had to play up their friendship in public, while Shadran reminded Gor that he had a small army of thugs at his disposal and Gor pointed out that he had a Roccarian warrior.

Careful. Maybe the dynamics I'm used to on Earth don't apply here. I chuckled at the idea. Some things were universal, and insincere protestations of friendship had to be one of them.

"And what is that beautiful morsel you bring to our home?" the furry figure asked, jabbing an arm in my direction. "Where did you find it? I didn't know there were such creatures on our island."

"Oh, that?" Kall Akkark would win no prizes for his acting. "Tch, it's just something we found on our way here. Too weak for the mines, but someone might give us a decent price for her as a plaything."

Vardok tensed by my side, like a volcano on the edge of an eruption. I brushed against him, and he subsided, but the fiery rage still radiated from him. Oblivious to the danger, the shaggy monster's grin widened, his eyes fixed on me as he replied.

"Ah, a lucky find. Yes, it is certainly worth something, and I can take it off your hands now to save you the trouble of shopping her around. Since we're such good friends, I can pay as much as five mega-zek."

I had no idea what that meant, but Vardok sucked in a deep breath. Something was wrong.

The Akkarks looked at each other meaningfully, and this time it was Gor who answered. "That's far too generous, old friend, but I'm afraid we can't take your money. We already have a buyer in mind, and I'm not keen to offend a client. Next time, maybe? I hate to disappoint a friend."

Shadran looked at me with dead eyes, his smile not touching them. Eyes I couldn't read, with no more empathy in them than a shark. I swallowed, wishing I could sink into the stone under me. *No, thank you, I don't want to stay here.*

A moment's tense pause stretched out for eons, and it felt like no one dared breathe. At last, and it had only been a second or two, Shadran laughed. "Of course, of course. Why, when one such prize falls into your laps, I'm sure another can't be far behind."

"And we'll be glad to offer you the next one first," Kall replied. All three of them lying. Just what was it about me they valued so much? I wasn't about to ask in front of everyone, and I wasn't even sure I wanted to know.

Chatting amiably, the three moved inside the

main building which towered over the courtyard, a door sliding open and spilling out light and warmth. As it slid shut behind them, Shadran's guards herded me and the chained slaves into a lightless room beside the gate and fasted the chain to a lock on the wall. Vardok snarled at the first to come near me, guiding me into the dark and leaning close to whisper.

"An automatic train runs from here to the mainland. It will leave before dawn." He squeezed my hand, and I swallowed nervously. "If you are on it, there's no way to recall it, and it will carry you to the Hub, where the main spaceport is."

"But what about—" Vardok cut me off before I could finish.

"I will join you if I can," he said, words that promised nothing. But the moment we'd had for talking was over and Vardok straightened up.

"She's secure," he told the guards, stepping outside. As the door swung shut, he caught my eye again.

Trust me, that look said. *I will protect you.*

And I did trust him. What choice did I have?

The guards swung the door shut, breaking our connection and leaving me in darkness with the other slaves. The ones that might want to kill me to spite the people who wanted to own me. What a pleasant thought. Even with them chained together and me free to move, there just wasn't anywhere to go to avoid them.

So use your words, dummy. Sensible Me could be pretty mean sometimes, but she had a point. I certainly couldn't fight them all.

"How are we going to get out of here?" I asked the nearest prisoner in a whisper. Maybe not the best opening gambit, but escape was the first thing on my mind. The train might be my way off the island, but how I'd reach it was anyone's guess.

He shrugged. "We'll get out of here when those bastards get up tomorrow. Another day and we'll reach the mines and that's it for us."

A mutter of dispirited agreement rose from the others, not one of them willing to take risk even discussing an escape. My chest tightened, and it took an effort to unclench my jaw and answer. "Shouldn't you be at least trying to get away?"

"Even if we could get out of these chains, where would we escape to? This island is dead, most of the plants are toxic from decades of pollution and the animals are half-starved and mad. The Blood Talons know everywhere that's habitable, and if we go back to the farms we came from, they'll raze them to the ground. Best we can hope for is that Shadran wants some more slaves around here, otherwise it's the mines for us."

"Slow death, there," another added in a musical voice. "At least here we'll live a while longer, perhaps long enough for things to change. Rebelling now? We'd all die."

"Don't know what you're worried about, human," a third alien said. "You won't be going to the mines. Play your cards right and you'll be comfortable while the korran ore dust rots our brains."

A hostile mutter ran around the group, and the hairs on the back of my neck stood up. They resented me, and now that we were all locked up together, I had no one to protect me. My only advantage if they decided to kill me was that they were all chained together, and I didn't know if that would slow them enough to keep them from catching me.

Maybe I should have let it go there and not risked antagonizing them further, but not knowing what was going on was too frustrating. I risked another question. "Why am I different? What makes me special to these bastards?"

The reaction surprised me. Stunned silence filled the room, the incredulous aliens seeming unable to understand my question. A couple of them even laughed, though the quick, sharp and humorless sounds held no joy and quickly faded to nothing.

I didn't know what to say, so I kept quiet until the tension got too much for one of them. "How do you not know? You are a *human female.*"

The emphasis made it clear I ought to know why that mattered, and my frustration boiled over. "Yes! Yes, I am, so what the fuck does that mean?"

Shocked noises filled the room. "How can you be so ignorant? Human females are universal breeders."

My turn to make a shocked sound. I tried to wrap my mind around those words and failed. Another of the alien slaves hissed in frustration, and I'd never identified with someone so much.

"How would she know, idiot? Humans come from a pre-space world, of course she doesn't understand."

"You think I keep track of where these things are from, tchel? Who has the time?"

"Just shut up and tell me," I said, my patience failing me. Someone at the back of the chain gang snickered, and the bickering stopped for a moment. I pushed on—there was nothing to gain by backing off now. "Please? I don't know what the hell is happening, or where I'm going, or *anything*. What on Earth is a universal breeder?"

That could have come out better, but maybe they'd respond to near-hysteria where reason failed? I wasn't too proud to play up my helplessness if it got me out of this mess.

"Your kind are universal breeders, a rare prize," the skinny lizard man said, slow and careful as though talking to a child. "You can breed with any species in the galaxy. Valuable anywhere, invaluable here. The Empire seeded this hell-hole with criminals of every species, mixed—finding a compatible female isn't easy, even for the rich and powerful. But a human? Compatible with anyone."

Blood drained from my face, and my jaw hung open. The world seemed to spin around me. Whatever vague ideas I'd had about my likely fate, broodmare to a crime lord had been no part of it. The world went hazy around the edges as I thought about the possibility, and I considered lying down and hoping I'd wake up back in bed at home with a hell of a dream to tell my friends about.

*No. Mercedes Lang, you are **not** giving up. Not while I have a say in the matter. No fainting for you!*

I took a deep breath, then another, waiting for my head to clear, hanging on to consciousness with a grim determination. If this was a dream, nothing I did mattered. If it was real, lying down and giving up wasn't my style.

"Fuck that," I said when I felt steady enough. "I'm going to find a way out. Hop the train to the mainland, get a ship, home. Easy."

"They will punish us all if one of us escapes," one of my cellmates protested. His neighbor hooted a quiet laugh.

"What are they going to do, send us to the korran mines?" A grim chuckle went up at that, and the tension lifted. The speaker waited for the laughter to die down before continuing. "You, human, good luck to you. The odds are long against you, but I want to see the looks on those bastards' faces if you get out of their clutches."

"Fine." The alien who'd protested sounded resigned rather than happy. "If you're going to do this, do it right. The platform is behind the citadel, you'll have to find a way through yourself. Five gods know what you'll do if you reach the Hub, but at least you'll be far from this hell."

The rest muttered agreement, and I felt touched. Even if they only cared that my escape would hurt their enemies, that was enough.

I LOVED MY BOOTS, but practical footwear for sneaking around an alien slave farm they were not. Every step I took, I dreaded making enough noise to attract attention, or finding some unseen obstacle by tripping over it. Twist an ankle here and there wouldn't be any recovering.

There weren't any guards watching the communal cell, thank goodness, and the door itself was unlocked. Perhaps Shadran didn't see the need for more security, or maybe he just had bigger threats to worry about—guards stood on a walkway at the top of the compound's wall, looking outward. A powerful urge to hurry before they looked around gripped me, but any noise risked drawing their attention, so I took things slowly and carefully, sticking to the darkest shadows.

The hard, unwelcoming architecture seemed designed to make me feel small as I crept through the darkness. To distract myself, I tried to work out what the various buildings were for. It reminded me of a medieval castle—the towering citadel obviously housed the baron and his knights, and the outer wall kept everyone else both safe from marauders and trapped at the baron's mercy. Aside from the materials, this wouldn't have been out of place in ancient Rome.

If it works, don't fix it, I guessed. There were some improvements, obviously. Electric lighting in the citadel, guards with guns rather than spears, and a high-tech lock on the outer gates. I didn't even know what a key for that would look like, which ruled out leaving that way. The walls were high enough to stop me considering jumping even before I thought about the guards who'd surely see me try.

My heart sank, and I saw why the other prisoners were so fatalistic. Getting out unseen was tough enough, but what then? I'd get a night's head start, if that, and then the hunters would start after me. Even if I avoided them, where would I go?

Don't think about that now. Take it one step at a time and get as far as possible. Even if I don't get away, I'll at least make them work for their prize.

And if there really was a train to catch, maybe I'd get clear of the Blood Talons after all. The only trouble was that I knew where the train station *wasn't.* I'd have seen the tracks if it had been on the side of the castle I came in on, which meant that it had to be on the far side of the citadel that loomed over me like an angry god.

It took me an age to reach the fortress, frightened

at every step that someone would hear me and come and investigate. Once there, I had to make a choice. The front door was a terrible idea, but it might be the best of a bad lot. At least I'd be inside, out of line of sight of the guards. For all I knew, though, there would be a guard right there on the far side. Or I could look for a stealthier way through, with every second a gamble that no one turned in my direction.

Cursing under my breath, I kept going. The door was too much of a risk, and there had to be another way in. None presented itself, though. The windows were too high to reach or too narrow to climb through. Next to a stairway up to the outer wall, I did find a small door recessed into the citadel concrete facade. Not that it helped—it was locked tight, which shouldn't have surprised me. Shadran wouldn't give rebellious slaves easy access to his throat, after all.

Beside the door, a narrow opening spilled light into night, and as I began to creep away, I heard a familiar clacking of beaks from it. Pausing, I decided to eavesdrop on the Akkarks' conversation. Knowledge is power, as someone said, though I couldn't remember who.

"Fuck heading back to the bosses, they won't give us half what she's worth. We grab the human, sneak aboard the train to the Hub." Gor spoke indistinctly around a mouthful of food. "She'll fetch a high price at auction, more than we'll ever make here. Enough to buy our ticket off this rock. The rest of the Talons can find their own humans."

I peeked in through the window, the narrow gap in the stonework giving me just enough space to see the two brothers at a table in a large kitchen. Simple but hearty food sat on the table, on counters, everywhere. My tummy rumbled—the Akkarks hadn't starved us on the march, but the flavorless bars of whatever they fed us did nothing to quell my appetite for proper food.

Fortunately, Kall's reply covered any noise I made. "What about the Roccarian and the other slaves? Can't take them with us."

Gor jabbed a fork in his brother's direction. "Of course not, idiot. We'll have to leave them behind."

"Shame to waste merchandise," Kall said, tearing chunks off a loaf. The smell of fresh bread was the finest thing I'd ever breathed, and honestly, I might have traded a future in the mines for an all-you-can-eat seat at that table. "Maybe Shadran will take them off our hands?"

"We can't let Four Arms know what a prize she is.

He's already suspicious, you saw. Besides, what are the few coins he'd throw us going to matter?"

"They'll matter if we need to pay someone before we can sell her," Kall said. His brother might call him a fool, but he had an eye for detail that I kind of admired.

"Not worth the risk of alerting Shadran." Gor waved off his brother's concerns. "He can have the lot of them."

"And Vardok?"

"Has to die, obviously. Can't leave him to chase after us, and as soon as we betray the Talons, he won't have a choice. He's tough, but we'll have the element of surprise and fight him two to one. The Roccarian will be dead before he knows he's in danger."

It was hard to explain the dread those words filled me with, making me sick to my stomach. Selling me to the highest bidder was awful, but I didn't expect better from slavers. Killing Vardok, though? Somehow that crossed a line in my mind I hadn't known about.

I withdrew into the shadows, unwilling to press my luck by eavesdropping any longer. If I was still here in the morning, Vardok would die.

I had to escape—not just for my sake, but for

his, too.

A noise behind me froze the blood in my veins and I kept as still as I could, praying the shadows would hide me. The stairs leading up to the wall creaked under heavy feet, and low voices carried to me, barely audible.

One of them sounded like Shadran, soft and delicate for such a huge monster. I didn't care about eavesdropping as long as they didn't notice me, so I would have stayed still and silent if I hadn't overheard one word clearly: *Vardok.*

It shouldn't have made any difference, but it did. Staying hidden was my best chance for escape, but I had to know what they were saying. Creeping closer, quiet as possible, I slipped under the wooden stairs, hiding among the barrels stored there, listening.

"Sir, are you sure?" A rough, gravelly voice asked. "Vardok isn't just a skilled warrior, he's property of the Blood Talons. Even if we kill him—"

"Not 'if,' Heras. When I command, you will slay him. Let me worry about the rest of the Talons," Shadran said, his quiet, silken voice no less menacing for its softness. "Kill the Roccarian and his masters, and you have a bright future ahead of you."

"Yes sir," the other alien said, and even I heard the doubt in his voice. But then he found his courage, or possibly remembered to sound confident in front of his boss. "We'll strike an hour before dawn. I don't care how fast a Roccarian's reflexes are, he can't dodge in his sleep."

Crap. Double crap. The pair wandered out of hearing range while I bit down on my hand to keep myself from screaming. Was *everyone* in this place backstabbing everyone else?

It's a den of slavers, Mercy. What the fuck did you expect from the scum who think they can own people? I tried to focus on what to do next. There had to be something, anything.

The idea of abandoning Vardok to be murdered was too awful to contemplate. But there was no way I could search the citadel for him. I briefly considered sounding an alarm, but it wouldn't do me any good to draw his attention if I got everyone else's, too. Lacking a better idea, I decided to keep looking for the train. Vardok said he'd meet me there, so I should at least know where it was.

By the time I had my breathing back under control, Shadran and his guard were out of sight. Cautiously emerging from the shadows, I climbed the stairs they'd come down, pressing myself against the rough concrete and hoping no one looked my way. Reaching the top of the wall where it met the citadel, I looked around carefully before stepping off the stairs.

To my right stood the citadel, a looming, imposing block of darkness. An alcove held another door inside, looking as heavy and secure as the one downstairs. On my left, the walkway extended along the outer wall, and I could just make out a guard further along. My heart skipped a beat, and I froze in place, watching him. His attention stayed fixed on the night outside the walls, and I breathed easier. As quietly as I could, I crossed the walkway to the parapet and looked down.

Yep. There was the train, all right. Long and sleek, it looked *fast* and I longed to find out how fast. Sneak aboard and wait for it to leave, zoom off into the distance with Vardok at my side and the wind in my hair. A beautiful, stupid daydream, and that was what it would remain unless I found a way down.

Which didn't look too likely. The wall was too high to jump down from safely, and sickly yellow lighting illuminated the train and platform. I'd be in plain view as I tried to find a way aboard the train, and at least one guard was watching the platform. The alternative was to keep looking for a safer way down, but I'd already pushed my luck further than I liked.

So—jump down and risk breaking a leg, or sneak off and hope I found an unguarded door to the train platform? Neither sounded good, but if there was a third choice, I couldn't see it.

I don't know how long I'd have stayed there dithering over my decision if fate hadn't taken a hand. The stairs creaked behind me, giving me warning that someone was on their way up, and I bit down on a curse. Choices: I could stay where I was and get caught for certain. Cross that off the list.

Jumping over the parapet would get me to the ground and out of sight of whoever was behind me. Of course, it would put me in view of the other guard, and I guessed I had a fifty-fifty chance of breaking a bone. Better than just waiting to be caught, but not by much.

That left one last, desperate option. The recessed door to the citadel was in heavy shadow, and maybe, if luck smiled on me, I could stay hidden in the darkness. It was a stupid plan, but better than the other two, so I crammed myself in tight against the door.

Just in time. The guard who'd talked with Shadran walked right past me as he returned to his post. Heras, Shadran had called him. I got a good look at him now, hunched forward with an alligator's snout stretched out, ready to bite at any second.

A long, heavy tail counterbalanced him, swishing from side to side as he walked, and he looked like a miniature T-Rex aside from a few details. His arms, adorned with Blood Talon tattoos, were too big for a dinosaur. And no T-Rex had ever worn a holster, complete with a massive laser pistol.

He didn't look in my direction, but that was all the good luck I got. His post turned out to be where I'd stood seconds ago, keeping watch on the train. He wasn't going anywhere anytime soon, and so neither was I. There was no way past him without attracting his attention. Staying put wasn't an option, either. All he needed to do was glance right, and he'd be looking right at me close enough to touch.

Only one possibility presented itself, and it was awful. One step and I'd be next to him, close enough to grab his pistol from his belt. If it was easy to use, if it didn't have a safety, if I could lift the damned thing, I'd shoot him before he reacted.

If the answer to any of those questions was 'no,' I was *fucked.*

Terrible plan, but what else did I have to work with? I took a deep breath, braced myself, and that was the moment a hand clamped down over my nose and mouth. *Crap.*

6

VARDOK

Sleep refused to come, no matter how hard I tried to relax. Shadran put me up in a nice room taken from one of his guards, which was suspicious—usually I stayed in the pen with the slaves, or with the Akkarks. Rather than object, the Akkark brothers had sent me up to get some rest. They never did that. Paranoid about their safety, they wanted me on hand at all times. Something was wrong, and yet each time I tried to figure out *what*, I got lost in thoughts of Mercy, the pretty, lost, human female.

As pleasant as thinking of her was, it didn't help me work out what to do. No matter what she looked like under those enticing black clothes, or how her lips would taste, she was out of my reach for now.

But telling myself that had no effect. The golden lines of my enhancements shimmered and burned, and any thought of sleep was laughable.

With a sigh, I heaved myself out of bed and paced the room. It was almost a joke: I rarely had a chance to sleep in a bed big enough for me, and now that I did, fate cursed me to stay awake. The sparsely furnished room was far more comfortable than I was used to, the floor covered with a thick, soft rug that deadened the sound of my footfalls. A small window let in the starlight, giving me plenty of light to see by.

A desk stood against one wall, a deactivated holo-display mounted on it. I assumed this was the guard commander's room, mostly because it had two doors. Who else would need quick access to both the citadel and the upper wall? I wondered what he thought about being kicked out of his bedroom for me? Like any other thought that wasn't about Mercy, it slipped away before I could properly consider it.

I'd never felt anything like this. Even before my capture, when my enhancements held me loyal to officers I'd chosen to serve, there'd been an edge of pain to remind me if I ever thought of disobeying. The price of my enhancements—they made me too dangerous to allow to roam free. Now, though, even when I thought about disobeying a direct order to go to Mercy, nothing happened.

No pain, no warning, just an urgent need to see her and hear her voice. Testing further, I walked to the outer door. No pain. Reached for the switch beside it. Nothing. Even thinking about killing the Akkarks and stealing Mercy only made me wince. Somehow, her presence overrode the programming that corrupted my enhancements. They responded as though she was the one person who mattered— and I didn't disagree.

Would it work on actions, or did she only protect my thoughts? If so, my options opened up. And I could test that easily enough. Kall had ordered me to go to my room and get some sleep, which made leaving the room an act of disobedience.

I pressed the door switch and braced myself for the inevitable searing pain to follow.

None came. Instead, the door slid soundlessly open, and I found myself staring at the back of Mercy's head. Past her, Guard Captain Heras, the man whose room I'd taken, stood looking out over the rail terminus. Mercy crouched, all her attention on the captain, gathering herself and about to leap into action. I didn't know what she had planned, but I didn't need to. If she picked a fight with that man, things would go badly whether she won or lost.

Before she could get herself killed, I reached around her, clamping my hand across her face and pulling her back into the room. My hearts thumped, and I held Mercy off the floor, both my arms wrapped around her and restraining her thrashing limbs. She got some solid hits in, which I ignored. Without leverage, the most she could do was make me feel the impacts.

Outside, Heras must have wondered if he'd imagined seeing something. Was it worth his time investigating? To my relief he chose not to, and after a long count of one hundred, I relaxed and lowered Mercy to the floor.

"If I let you go, will you keep quiet?"

She nodded. I let go. She spun and punched me.

That strike was better. Someone had taught her well, and she put all her weight and strength through the first two knuckles of her right fist and straight into my solar plexus.

Taken by surprise, I staggered back, and Mercy followed, aiming an uppercut at my jaw. Her form was good, but she was no warrior—I had all the time I needed to catch her wrist and guide her arm aside. That put her off balance, and I didn't give her a chance to recover, knocking her legs out from under her and sending her to the floor with a thump.

We both froze, looking at the door. No one knocked, no one barged in, no one, it seemed, cared. I relaxed again, though this time I kept a closer eye on Mercy.

"What are you doing here? Why are you fighting me?"

"What the fuck, Vardok? What do you expect, grabbing me from behind and dragging me into your lair?"

She pulled herself up onto her elbows, gasping for breath and glaring daggers at me. *Almost* at me, rather. The room was too dark for her to see me, but that wasn't going to stop Mercy. It was adorable, though I knew better than to tell her that—I'd get another punch for my troubles, if I was any judge.

"I saved your life, most likely. If Heras had spotted you out of the slave quarters without permission, they'd have nailed you to the doors alive as a warning to the others."

Mercy's lips compressed into a tight line, her glare intensifying. "I was going to escape, asshole, and you know I'm too valuable to kill. I'm valuable enough to steal, after all."

"Don't bet your life on that," I said, before the last

words registered. Then it was my turn to frown. "What do you mean, steal?"

She swallowed. "I overheard Shadran giving the orders. His men are going to kill you, then the brothers, and he'll keep me for himself. I don't know what he's planning past that, but I don't care."

I straightened immediately, turning to the door, my mind racing. "An honorless tchel, to murder guests under his roof."

"It's not like they're any better," Mercy said. "I overheard them, too. They're planning on killing you and taking me for themselves."

"Those half-digested fools," I rumbled, wondering why that surprised me. Criminals turning out to be untrustworthy should not be a shock. "I should have seen that coming. Those two may be part of the gang, but they have no loyalty except to each other and their profits."

"What are we going to do?" Mercy's voice shook, as well it might. We were alone, without allies and amongst enemies. Despair would be easy, but my rage held it at bay. How dare these fools frighten my Mercy? I'd tear out their hearts and make an offering of them to her.

But right now, she needed reassurance rather than a bloody reckoning. "I will do the simple, obvious thing. Kill them all and take the trip to the Hub ourselves. There are ships there, I can get you off planet and on your way home."

"You really think you can do that?" She didn't sound confident. Fair enough, I wasn't sure I could do it, either. Shadran had his guards, and the Akkarks were tough. Tax collectors for the Blood Talons had to be. I'd never fought that many people at once. "I thought you couldn't defy them?"

"I couldn't, before." I turned to watch one of the three moons crest the horizon, feeling my way through the words as I said them. "But you are my mate, and we are linked by that. The mate bond is everything to a Roccarian, and it overrides my other programming."

Turning back, I looked at her again, letting my emotions rise again. There were many enemies, all intent on doing her harm, and only one of me. The fight would be desperate. It didn't matter. I refused to flinch from my duty to my mate.

"I will slay them all for you," I said, letting my anger hide my worries. "No matter what, you shall be free. I swear it on my life."

7

MERCY

hat little starlight spilled in through the window did little to illuminate the room, and after fumbling my way onto the bed. I stayed put rather than risking running into something. Vardok was no more than a shadow in the darkness, pacing back and forth.

Either he could see in this light, or he did a damned good impression of it. He prowled the room like a hungry predator, keeping his distance from me. Almost like he didn't want to risk being close to me in case he lost control.

Maybe I wouldn't mind if he did. I tried to shake off that thought and focus on more important things.

"What are we going to do?" I kept my voice low.

The last thing we needed was to draw attention. "I mean, do you have a plan, Vardok?"

A muffled chuckle. "Always. But then you came along and ruined them all."

I felt my cheeks heat and hoped the darkness hid my blush. "Okay, do you have a *new* plan, now that I've fucked up your old one?"

A weighty pause followed, and I'd almost given up on getting an answer when he spoke again. "I have parts of a plan, yes."

"Let me guess. Step one, kill everyone who's a danger to you. Step two, get me safely home. Step one's the bit that needs work."

"...that is roughly accurate, yes, though I intend to kill those who threaten *you*."

Every other time I'd heard a promise like that, I'd been more frightened of the man making the offer than whoever he was offering to beat up. Vardok's promise of violent protection was different—it made me feel *safe*. Unlike the human men, I knew Vardok would never turn that anger and violence on me.

How I knew was a question I didn't have an answer to, but that didn't keep me from believing it. And right now, I didn't have any choice. If there was a non-violent solution to my problems, it was well hidden.

Determined to get some more satisfying answers, I pressed him. "How are you going to fight all of them? And what do I do?"

"You will stay here and keep out of danger," Vardok said. It wasn't a suggestion. He meant for me to obey, and that did complicated things to my emotions. On the one hand, I made my own decisions. On the other, his powerful dominant attitude pushed my buttons in ways I'd never have expected, and I squirmed as a tingling sensation spread through me.

While I tried to think of something to say, Vardok kept speaking. His voice came slow, thoughtful, and I realized he was making his plan up as he went. "I will lay an ambush. If they intend to start by killing me, I shall be where they expect me, ready to spoil their day before it begins."

That made me feel better. I'd worried that he'd leave me on my own while he fought my battle for me, and then what would I do if the guards came here? Aside from that, being alone with Vardok in the dark room was exciting in a different, more pleasant way. Perhaps my mind just didn't want to think about the killing that would happen soon, but I couldn't help thinking of the feel of Vardok's alien skin and wonder what it would be like to kiss his strong, rugged face, to feel his lips on mine.

We waited in silence for what felt like hours, though I doubt more than thirty minutes passed while I watched him. Or tried to—Vardok was a shadow against the blackness, and I only had a loose impression of where he was. If he'd stood still, I'd have lost him completely, but he paced up and down like a caged tiger, and the faint starlight was just enough to see his movement.

"Can we turn on the light?" I asked, the tension becoming unbearable. "I can't see anything."

"With the light on, Heras may think I'm awake," Vardok said. "It will spoil the ambush."

I pulled a face but didn't argue. As much as I wanted to see him, it wasn't worth risking our lives for. Resigning myself to a long night of being too tense to sleep and too tired to think, I didn't notice the golden light glimmering in the darkness at first. It brightened, becoming unmissable as it spread in wavy patterns twisting around Vardok.

The gold markings on his skin, I realized belatedly. My alien warrior was *glowing*.

The trails of gold that marked Vardok's skin shone with light, soft enough that I could look straight at it and, as my eyes adjusted, see the rest of him in that dim light. I stared, mouth falling open, and he stifled a laugh at my shock.

"You," I told him as sternly as I could, "are naked."

It was so obvious as to not be worth saying, but somehow, I needed to. The golden lines forming a pattern around his body hid nothing from view, and wow did Vardok have nothing to hide.

His muscular legs were as gorgeous as the rest of him, lean and subtly alien, putting him naturally on the balls of his feet and ready to pounce or chase. The light winding around him showed off all his muscles to best effect, making him irresistibly attractive. The play of light and shadow across his abs made my body quiver and short-circuited something in my brain.

As much as I tried to keep myself from ogling, resistance was impossible. My gaze inevitably made its way along the paths of light to his cock.

His *impossibly huge* cock. Perhaps, I told myself, it was the light? Glowing lines ran along and around the erect shaft and maybe made him look bigger than he was. My cheeks burned as I thought, *I guess I'll have to take a closer look.*

I'd thought Vardok was gorgeous before, but now he was the most beautiful person I'd ever seen. I wanted to pounce on him *right now.*

No. That wasn't quite right. I wanted Vardok to pounce on me, not the other way round. Taking a deep breath to steady myself, I did my best to stop staring, or at least look him in the face. For the first time since I'd met him, he sported a happy smile. A proud smile, even.

He deserved it. Just looking at him took my breath away.

Moving toward me, he seemed to glide across the thick carpet, making no sound at all. None I could hear over the pounding of my pulse, anyway. I stood, swallowing as he towered over me.

It hadn't been a trick of the light—he really was that big. I bit my lip, reaching out to touch his cock and then pausing, my breath ragged.

"We shouldn't," I said. "What if they come for you?"

"If they haven't come yet, they won't until morning." Vardok spoke with such authority that I didn't doubt him for a moment. He knew these aliens. If he said it, it must be true. Right?

That was why I believed him, and not because I wanted him to touch me so very, very desperately. And I knew no one would be fooled by that line, not even myself.

Another step took him inside my personal space,

and my skin tingled. I realized I was chewing on my lip as I stared at him. Scared and excited in equal amounts by the sheer size of him, I reached out unsteadily to touch Vardok's cock and trace the golden lines.

He gasped, growled, tensed. Holding himself back as I ran my fingers down his shaft, gently caressing and gasping as his cock stiffened and grew. It felt like a thinly padded rod of iron, pulsing oddly in my hand, and I could barely get my hand around it.

It's too big, I thought, more awed than scared. However big it was, I *needed* to feel it inside me, to know how the strange, rough-smooth texture felt filling me. I slipped from my place on the bed, sinking down to my knees so that I could kiss his shaft.

The result was more than anything I'd have imagined. Vardok's entire cock *vibrated,* the pattern of lights pulsing fast against my fingers. I experimented again, running my tongue up his shaft and around the head of his cock, and the vibrations intensified. I squirmed, pressed my legs together, and wondered what it would be like inside me.

There was only one way to find out, and I knew it. But the anticipation was so sweet, and there was still an edge of fear to the idea, so I drew it out a little longer. Ducking my head, I kissed the tip of his cock before sliding it between my lips. I almost couldn't take him into my mouth, he was so big, but I managed and the fierce growl of pleasure I won from him sent an answering shudder of joy through me.

Vardok's hand cupped the back of my head and he guided me with surprising gentleness. I felt the strength in his grip, knew I was helpless against it, and knew the effort he put into keeping himself in check. Sure his control wouldn't last, I savored the strange texture of his skin, the warmth, the weird vibration against my tongue. And then slowly drew back, looking up the mountain of muscles to meet his gaze.

"My turn," he said, baring his teeth in a predator's grin that sent a jolt of fear and anticipation through me. Before I could respond, he lifted me onto the bed, pushed my dress up past my hips, and tore my panties from me. I gasped as he pushed my legs apart, rough but careful, and knelt between them. Gasped again as his lips, then teeth, grazed my inner thighs, alternating sides and slowly, so damned slowly, worked their way up.

If I'd teased him with my mouth, God, he

tortured me with his. Each tiny bite left a buzz of joy between my legs, merging as he added more and more, making me arch before he'd even touched my pussy. I bit back the pleas I wanted to shout at him, refusing to show weakness. And trying not to attract the guards' attention. I could pretend that was the reason, but in the heat of the moment I'd almost forgotten about them.

Reaching down, I grabbed his head, my fingers sliding into his thick hair and pulling, trying to steer him. Without stopping his kisses, he looked up at me, mischief shining in his eyes, and he *slowed down.* I groaned, delicious frustration making my hips buck until he grabbed them and steadied me.

And brought his mouth to my pussy, eagerly licking and kissing. And wherever his tongue touched, waves of pleasure rippled out through my body. It wasn't simply skill, enthusiasm, or energy. Something else about him drove me wild, something I couldn't identify and wouldn't mind if it took hours—*days*—of experiments to understand.

Vardok wouldn't mind that, I thought. From the way he growled hungrily into me, he was delighting in the taste of me. I threw my head back, grabbed a pillow, and covered my face to stifle a cry of pleasure as he licked me into an orgasm that nearly blew the top of my head off.

I'd never felt anything like it. There should have been lights, a fanfare, banners announcing Vardok champion or something. Maybe those all happened —I wouldn't have noticed.

And Vardok hadn't finished with me yet.

Lifting me by the hips, he pulled me to him. Weak as I was, I still wrapped my legs around him and stared up at him. The golden lines glowed and pulsed in time with his heartbeats as he pressed the rigid, ridged length of his cock against my pussy.

His grin could have eaten worlds. I groaned, reaching out for him, stroking his cock and positioning him, but still, he didn't move. And I knew what he wanted.

"Please," I whimpered. I'd never wanted, *needed*, anything so much in my life. Vardok needed it as much as I did, but still he held himself back.

"What is it you need, my love?" His rumbling growl vibrated through me, and I shuddered. "Tell me what you desire."

"I need you, I need you inside me. *Please.*"

Either that was what he'd been waiting for, or it was enough to break his self-control. His thrust was smooth, powerful, and deep. Holding my hips tight, he pulled me in to meet him and buried his monster cock to the hilt.

The sensation was incredible. I threw my head back, grabbed the bedsheets, and would have shouted my pleasure to the world if I could. It wasn't choice that kept me quiet—the sensation was just too much for me and I nearly stopped breathing.

Which would have been a hell of a way to die, but worth it.

Vardok thrust hard, again and again, and each time I felt the strange, wonderful, alien texture of his cock sliding in and out. Felt the heat of him inside me, his size stretching me, the vibrations building as he fucked me better than I'd ever imagined anyone could.

The first orgasm came quickly as waves of pleasure crashed through my body like tidal waves. They caught me up, carrying me into a white-hot climax that left me weak and trembling.

"Vardok," I said as soon as I could speak again. It came out a gasp.

"Mercy," he replied, voice rougher, darker than before. Possessive, intense, and wonderful—just hearing my name said like that pushed me over the edge again. I squeezed him inside me, my pussy holding him as though I'd never let go.

He leaned in, kissing me on the breasts, his dexterous tongue darting out to lick my nipples and leave them alight with pleasure. Bit his way up to my neck. I tried to speak, but even I didn't know what I wanted to say.

My alien lover understood well enough, though. Our lips met in a kiss that set off an explosion of pleasure, his tongue pressing into my mouth and dancing with mine. More and more urgent, he pounded me into the bed, and I lost track of everything that wasn't him. Vardok was my whole universe, and I lost track of where I ended and he began.

He swelled inside me, stretching me, vibrating against me, and I felt his orgasm like an oncoming wave. My own rose to meet it, and the world melted into light. Vardok growled into the kiss, I cried out, both of us lost in the incredible ecstasy we brought each other.

FINE LINES of gold stretched across my skin, marking me and linking me to the alien in my arms as we floated amongst the stars. They lay beneath us like a river in the night sky, and above us like a protective dome. Nothing and no one could reach us here, so I smiled and snuggled into Vardok's arms.

And then my eyes opened. Confusion swept over me as, only half-awake, I tried to separate dream from reality. Obviously, I wasn't floating down a river of stars with my alien lover. That was crazy. But equally obviously, this wasn't my apartment. It wasn't my bed. And I wasn't alone.

Did I hook up with someone last night? That wasn't like me at all, but the last thing I remembered was Emily's hen night. After that... the whole alien planet thing had to be a dream, right? Though hopefully my subconscious based it on the guy in bed with me. He was big and muscular enough, and I felt appropriately worn out. Sore even, though it was a pleasant ache.

Inventory. No hangover, good but weird. My mouth, breasts, and thighs tingled strangely. Not unpleasant, in fact the opposite, but not something I'd felt before. That pulled me more awake as I tried to pin it down, and the only thing I could think was drugs.

Which was also so not me. Had this guy drugged me? Was that why I'd had such weird dreams? Maybe that thought should have freaked me out, but it didn't—somehow, I felt sure that this man hadn't slipped me anything. If drugs were the cause of those weird dreams, they were drugs I'd taken willingly.

Part of me insisted they were memories, not dreams. I told it to shut up and stand in the corner. Being abducted by aliens was a lot less likely than meeting a guy and trying some drugs, wasn't it?

But I remembered the dream more clearly than the party. I tried to disentangle myself from the sheets and slip out of bed without him noticing, but as soon as I sat up, a powerful arm pulled me back against the solid, muscular form of the man behind me.

"Mercy," he whispered, voice low, rough, alien—but familiar. My breath caught as I admitted to myself that this was real, that I'd really slept with an alien. I'd had *the best sex of my life* with an alien.

"Vardok," I whispered back, wondering what happened next. My body had a few suggestions for that, but as tempting as it was to give in and jump Vardok, I didn't dare. I had no idea how long I'd slept, and Shadran's guards could arrive to murder us at any moment. At least they'd been polite enough to stay away while Vardok had his wonderfully wicked way with me.

"How long have I been asleep?"

Vardok shrugged, the muscles of his chest contracting behind me, and I couldn't help snuggling back against him. He let out a little growl, and I shivered at that predatory sound.

I didn't mind being this alien's prey, not one bit.

"You slept half the night. You needed it."

"Hey, you've been awake as long as I have. Maybe longer."

"I am a Roccarian. I will sleep when I need to, and not while you are in danger. No power in the universe would keep me from watching my mate sleep and making sure you wake safely."

From any other man, that would have sounded nice but empty. Vardok, though, meant every word and could follow through on his promise. And I couldn't deny how welcome that was. Confused, afraid, and apparently on another fucking planet, I took comfort in his solid and caring embrace.

He held me close, close enough to feel the twin heartbeats in his chest, a soothing, almost hypnotic sound. My eyes shut, I snuggled into him, holding on as though he was the only solid thing in my life, and drifted back into sleep.

8

VARDOK

Mercy's head rested on my chest, and my arm folded under her, holding her to me. If I could have stayed there forever, I would have. Unfortunately, I had to move, to prepare for the assassins Mercy had warned me about.

The thought hurt—not in the physical way my enhancements punished me for disloyalty, but a worse pain in my soul. If the Akkarks took my Mercy to the Hub for sale, the vilest scum of the galaxy would be there to bid for her. I had no desire to think about what they might do to her.

Delivering her to the Blood Talons' lair would be no better. The gang's brutal leadership would either sell her or, worse still, keep her for their own amusement. And Shadran would be as bad as any other Blood Talons leader if his plan to steal her worked.

Mercy would not suffer the fate of being abused so, not while I drew breath. I'd kill them all first.

Long experience made me brace for the pain that thought should have brought, but nothing happened. No burning pain, no punishment, not even a twinge. My human mate's touch had freed me of the curse laid on my enhancements. No matter what hacks the Imperial technicians had worked, no Roccarian technology would prioritize anything over a warrior's mate. Or so I hoped.

"I'll know soon enough," I said under my breath, hearing movement outside, the careful tread of warriors creeping into position to strike. Warriors who weren't nearly as stealthy as they thought they were—in the still night, they'd have been better off rushing in and giving me less time to react.

Leaving Mercy with a quick kiss on her forehead, I slipped out of bed and crept toward the door. The thick carpet swallowed any sound my footsteps made, and the darkness hid me well. Unlike my foes, I knew the art of stealth and night-fighting. I'd soon teach them a lesson, though I didn't intend for any to survive to learn from it.

The door slid open silently, letting in the chill

night air along with the starlight. Three guards entered, led by Heras, slow and careful not to make a sound. I waited until they were all inside and turning their weapons toward the bed.

Now my enhancements sent warning pain through my nerves, though I didn't need the prompt. No one would point a gun in the direction of my beloved and live.

I stepped into the patch of light, a deliberately heavy step that brought the three guards spinning round to face me. I struck as they moved, my claws digging into the throat of the middle guard and tearing it out before he'd turned half way.

Blood sprayed and plasma guns roared, but I'd already darted back into the shadows. Blinding-bright lines of light tore across the room, blasting the desk to pieces and leaving a hole in the wall beside the door. Not in me, though, and the blasts had ruined everyone's night vision.

I didn't need to see to find my enemies. They were noisy enough to hunt blind, and while they had good instincts and training, mine were better. As the two ducked away from the doorway, seeking safety in the darkness, I pounced again. Striking the remaining guard head on, I bore him to the ground and bit at his neck. He twisted aside at the last moment and I got a mouthful of shoulder instead, while Heras took another wild shot above my head. He obviously didn't mind shooting his followers if that meant getting me, too.

The guard underneath me didn't like that. Abandoning his attempt to escape my grip, he kicked out into the dark and swept Heras's legs out from under him. With an outraged squawk, the captain came slamming down to our level, still clinging to his plasma pistol.

I didn't waste the opportunity, abandoning the injured and disarmed warrior and leaping at his commander. I grabbed hold of the pistol with one hand and slammed Heras' head into the floor with the other.

He roared in pain, long snout opened wide and showing off his sharp and menacing teeth. Pinning him took all my attention, and his surviving follower scrambled to his feet, dashing out of the room and howling for help.

"You can't fight us all," Heras said, his face a vicious snarl. My only answer was to lift his head and bring it down again with all my weight behind it. Even the luxurious carpet wasn't enough to protect his skull from that, and Heras fell silent.

Too late to stop the alarm from being raised. The

clanging of a bell, loud enough to wake the dead, replaced the runner's voice. Soon every guard in the compound would converge on us—unless I drew them away.

"Hide," I called out to Mercy, pulling a plasma pistol from the corpse of one of the fallen guards and lobbing it in her direction. "Hide, and only use that if you have to."

"No *fucking* way," Mercy said, catching the pistol. It might have looked comically big in her hands, but the spark of anger in her eyes drained any humor from it. Good. She looked ready and willing to use the gun if needed. "I'm coming with you. I don't want us kept apart for one second more than necessary."

A frustrated snarl escaped my lips. "I can move faster on my own, and I must find the Akkarks and Shadran. If they live to tell the rest of the Blood Talons what happened here, they'll send all their strength after us. Too many for the two of us to fight, and we cannot outrun them. Hide until the guards are distracted, then get to the train. I will meet you there."

Mercy stared at me, hesitating a moment too long before nodding. "Fine. But don't you dare get yourself killed or I swear I'll haunt you."

Not sure how serious that threat was, I nodded gravely. "I have no intention of dying, not now. I finally have something to live for."

Before she could respond, I turned and raced through the inner door, seeking my prey.

9

MERCY

ardok vanished into the citadel, leaving me alone in the bedroom, and my heart sank. It was easy to be confident when he was with me, but without him, I felt weak and vulnerable.

"Stop that," I told myself, trying to think what Vardok would say if he stood next to me. "I'm more than that. I'm a weak and vulnerable human *with a plasma gun.*"

That gave me enough of a boost to look for a hiding place. The room didn't offer much, but I found enough space under the bed. Grabbing my clothes and the gun, I crammed myself in there and tried to squirm into my dress and boots. I'd hardly started when someone burst through the outside door.

Frozen in place, I knew I'd come *this* close to death. Huge booted feet, all I could see of the guard, stomped around the room, and I prayed he wouldn't think to look under the bed.

To be fair, I didn't think Vardok would have fitted. The thought of him trying to hide here, his every breath lifting the bed, flashed into my mind and I struggled not to laugh. Hysterics would get me caught, and if I started laughing, I didn't know if I'd be able to stop.

"Not here," the alien shouted as more barreled in through the door. Sharp snaps echoed, the horrible sound of alien weapons firing somewhere in the building. The aliens cursed and followed the sound, leaving me alone to take a deep breath.

The smart thing to do was obvious. I'd be safe under the bed, and even if someone found my hiding spot, the plasma gun I cradled in my arms would give them a nasty surprise. I could stay here until the coast was clear or Vardok came back for me.

Looking up at the bedframe, I did my best to think through my near-panic. Something was wrong but figuring out *what* wasn't easy when the sporadic gunfire kept making me jump. Vardok would win his fight meet me at the train, or if I wasn't there, he'd know to look here. We'd escape to the Hub and then back to Earth…

…leaving the rest of the enslaved aliens to their fate. Damn. No, I couldn't let that happen. I *wouldn't* let it happen. With the guards busy hunting down Vardok, they'd never have a better chance to get free.

At least, that's what I told myself as I crawled out from under the bed. A careful peek outside showed an empty courtyard, now illuminated by harsh emergency lights. My heart hammered in my chest as I slowly took a step out into the open.

No shout of alarm, no volley of plasma fire to cut me down. Both promising signs. I pressed on, hurrying down from the wall and wishing the place was still cloaked in shadows. At least the lighting meant that I'd see any guards, though that was scant comfort. A flicker of motion at the far side of the farmhouse might have been a guard, or it might have been a bird. Or nothing more than my imagination, it was impossible to tell.

Dumping stealth in favor of speed, I ran for the door I'd sneaked out of earlier. One last look around and I pulled the door just wide enough to slip inside, pulling it closed behind me.

"You came back," someone said. After the near-blinding light outside, it was too dark to see anyone, but I made out some motion in the blackness toward the back of the barn. Walking in that direction, slowly so I didn't trip, I realized I should have thought about what I'd say now. I'd just have to improvise.

"That's right, I did. Now, who wants to be free?" As though to punctuate my words, a series of blasts cracked outside, followed by a scream. "Vardok's rebelling against the Blood Talons—you'll never have a better chance."

The quiet of the barn dissolved into a dozen people speaking at once, a cacophony that I couldn't understand. "Quiet down! The guards are busy, so I came back here free you. After that, what you do is up to you. There's a train ready to leave for the Hub, if you get on it you can hitch a ride off the island— but *I'm* going to help Vardok kill those fucking slavers."

The room erupted into a chaotic maelstrom of questions, all of which I ignored. There was no time for debate, even if I had been able to pick individual questions out of the chaos. I advanced carefully into the dark until I all but ran into the bound aliens. Hands caught me and I flinched away, but all they did was guide me forward until I reached the post they were all chained to. An expectant hush fell over the group.

"You've stolen the key?" I don't know who spoke, but her voice was like a song bird's.

"In a manner of speaking," I said. "Everyone close your eyes and look away."

I followed my own advice, and the glare of plasma still left bright spots dancing in front of my eyes. When I opened them again the heavy iron lock was simply gone.

The aliens wasted no time in pulling their cuffs free of the remains of the chain. They reached out for me again, this time whispering thanks as they touched me.

It made me tear up, or perhaps that was the after-effect of the plasma blast. Yep, sure, that was it. I didn't have time to get emotional.

"Okay, I'm going to help Vardok," I said. "Who's with me?"

"All of us." The same song-bird voice, speaking with absolute certainty. "You've given us a chance at freedom, and we will repay that debt."

VARDOK

The fortress was old, its bleak concrete built to house prison guards before the Empire left. The corridors, stark and cold and bare, were designed to be unwelcoming and intimidating, and it worked. When I first arrived, I wouldn't have believed it could house something worse.

No matter how low I set the bar, the Blood Talons had a talent for tunneling under it. The blocky corridors were now home to a garrison of slavers, the walls showed the scars of plasma burns, and most of the lighting had failed. At least the garrison was mostly asleep, but the alarm echoed down the halls, and *no one* would sleep through that.

A door to my left opened as I passed it, revealing a bleary-eyed Tovan still struggling with his blaster harness. He stopped dead, staring at my plasma gun, and I pulled the trigger without a second thought.

Blinding bright in the dim corridor, the plasma left a hole in his torso I could fit my fist through. I left him to fall back into his room, racing away before anyone else responded to the sound of the shot.

Luck favored me, or perhaps fate paid me back for the years of suffering I'd endured. No one else got in my way before I reached the stairwell, though I heard pursuit behind me. Taking the steps three at a time, I gambled the Akkarks were still where Mercy had seen them and raced toward the kitchens.

If they'd gone to their room, I would never find them in time. But I knew the brothers—they'd once spent a full day and a night feasting, and tonight they thought they had something to celebrate. As long as there was food and wine left, they'd stay put.

Bursting through the door, I barreled into a scene of pandemonium. Yes, Kall and Gor were there, standing by a table with the remains of a feast spread everywhere. Two Railhead guards lay amidst the chaos, one with his throat slit, the other with a cleaver lodged in his head. Three more still stood, warily watching the two brothers with drawn knives. The Akkarks hadn't gone unscathed, though

—Kall had a nasty cut to his shoulder and Gor's left hand dripped blood.

Instinct took over, and long training. I'd come here to kill the brothers, yes, but I'd also spent long years protecting them. And it was one thing to kill in order to save my mate. These five were here to murder a guest under their roof.

All that flickered through my mind in the time it took to squeeze the trigger again, sending a searing blast of light to cut down the nearest guard.

"Cowards," I said into the deathly silence that followed. "Two to one odds to murder your guests— and still you fail."

This was the first time I'd seen the Akkarks genuinely pleased to see me. Nothing like an assassination attempt to make people appreciate their bodyguards, even sociopathic gangsters.

"Vardok! You're alive," Kall cried out, and it sounded for all the world like he'd worried about my safety. "Kill the traitors, then we'll get out of here."

The remaining assassins rushed me without hesitation. It was their only choice—if they kept their distance, I'd pick them off with my pistol. If they attacked the Akkarks, Gor and Kall were skilled enough fighters to keep them busy while I moved in for the kill.

So they charged, and I rejoiced. One step to the left, putting one between me and his partners, and I lashed out, my claws extended.

The guard let out a high-pitched cry, which told me my claws hadn't slit his throat as I'd intended. Blood poured from his neck, and he backed off frantically, slamming into his larger companion and tangling them both with a chair.

I followed my prey, pouncing before they could catch their balance. This time my claws struck home, and while I tore his throat out, the Akkarks threw themselves on the others. They were despicable monsters, but there was nothing wrong with their combat skills. By the time I joined them, their foes were bleeding from a dozen stab wounds and no danger to anyone.

We stood over the rapidly dying bodies and looked at each other, blood spattered and out of breath. I could have killed them there, but I hesitated. We'd just fought together—it felt wrong to slay them without warning.

"We have to get out of here," Kall said, breaking the silence. "Grab the human and run. If we can get to the train—"

"*If.* I don't like hanging my survival on an if, brother."

"You think I do? What choice do we have? We can't give her to Shadran and hope he spares us. You know he'd kill us rather than let us go to plot our revenge."

For once, Gor didn't have an answer to his brutish brother. Clever planners like him had a weakness—they're always sure that, when things went wrong, they'd come up with a solution if they just thought hard enough. Thugs like Kall had the advantage there, resorting to violence instantly. It might not be the best course of action, but it *was* action. It might work, where sitting around thinking of the perfect response never would.

I'd come to kill the pair of them, but the way they looked at me as their only ally kept me from pulling the trigger. And a moment was all it took. Shadran's voice called from outside, amplified enough to wake the dead.

"I see my guards failed to kill you. A pity, those were some of my best men, and I've no desire to throw away more on this farce. Come out now, peaceable-like, and I'll forget our little misunderstanding. You can go on your way, with no hard feelings. If you make me come in there, though, I'll carve all three of you up and let the beasts feast on your guts you while you're still alive."

I grimaced. He had the numbers, he had the weapons, and he wasn't fool enough to waste them on a mindless charge. Attacking into the building would lessen those advantages, but he had time on his side and could wait for the right moment.

"I'm not one to trade a chance at life for a merciful death," Gor called out, helping himself to a heavy cleaver as he spoke. "So, what exactly are you offering, and why should I trust you to keep your word?"

"Because I'm no fool and won't throw my men away in a fight we can avoid. Awake, your Roccarian is too much trouble to kill."

I grinned at that, though no one would mistake my expression for 'friendly.' Kall ignored the negotiations, searching for more effective weapons than the half-dozen knives he'd already stuck through his belt. I joined him, and together we pulled the cooker's side panel open and dismounted the heavy battery inside.

Not much of a weapon, but something. Those industrial batteries packed a hell of a bang in the right circumstances. And if nothing else, it was a solid lump of metal with a handle.

"Okay, okay, here, I'll make it formal-like," Shadran said, still trying to talk us into stepping out into the killing zone outside. "I'll swear, if you come out peaceful, you'll not be harmed. I'll take the human girl, and that's it. Swear on my ancestors, may they eat my soul if I break this bond."

The Akkark brothers looked at each other and shared a disgusted noise that might have been a laugh if someone drowned it. I didn't think much of Shadran's oath, either, not without some leverage to make him keep it.

Kall obviously thought the same as me. "Let them come in. If they're going to kill us, no reason to make it easy for them."

Gor nodded absently, still deep in thought. I held little hope that he'd come up with anything. Boxed in as we were, there was no clever trick to win this fight.

At least I didn't drag Mercy into this, I thought. *Maybe she'll see the chance to escape—if she's ever going to get away, it's while Shadran's guards are busy here.*

We let the silence drag until the waiting guards grew restless and even Shadran realized his gambit wasn't working. The attack came unannounced, a reed-thin warrior pulling the door open to dart inside as his comrades leaned around the doorframe to fire at us.

Reed ran headlong into my blaster shot, Kall

threw a knife with deadly accuracy into one shooter, and a second took the battery to the face courtesy of Gor. Behind us, more warriors stormed the room from inside the citadel. A neat pincer maneuver which would have worked better if we hadn't already forced the attackers outside to back off.

If the two forces had coordinated their strikes, we'd have had no chance to fight them off. As it was, we whirled and charged into them, and they stalled in the face of our counterattack.

It couldn't last, though. For a moment, it was the three of us against the world, and I even felt a pang of regret that the Akkarks would die here. Hacking and slashing with cleavers and kitchen knives, they gave a good account of themselves.

I tore into the foe, blood spraying around me where I ripped flesh. The fight might be futile, but they'd pay a price for my death that they wouldn't soon forget.

Shouts from behind us alerted me that the outside forces had regrouped, certain that we had no way to resist them now. They were almost right.

Whirling, I raised my blaster, accepting a nasty cut across my back as the price of the shot. The guards charged through the doorway at us, stun-sticks raised and ready, and I'd only have one chance to fire before they were on me.

One was all I needed. The blinding line of plasma burned past the guards, hitting the battery lying beside the door and releasing its stored energy. The explosion filled the room with blue-white light and a sound like a meteor strike.

That ought to be enough of a signal for Mercy to get clear, I thought. Then something hit my skull, and everything went dark.

I WASN'T OUT LONG. My enhancements wouldn't allow it, even if waking me up damaged my nervous system. Better that than being killed while unconscious. Even with that help, the room spun around me when I opened my eyes.

The blast left a hole where the door had been, and corpses littered the room. Hard to count how many in the carnage, but it was easy enough to see that there weren't enough here to account for all of Shadran's guards. Half at most, between this and the ones I'd killed upstairs. Shapes moved in the smoke outside, more guards emerging to look at the destruction. They hesitated at the threshold, seeing the torn and crushed remains of their fellows.

Slavers, I thought with a grim smile. *Tough and mean in the face of unarmed and cowed slaves. They aren't used to meeting dangerous opposition.*

Shadran himself followed, pushing his reluctant guards forward. Like the Akkarks, he was one of the old guard, a prisoner who'd been part of the Blood Talon takeover of the island. He had many faults, but cowardice wasn't one of them.

Where's my plasma pistol? I fumbled at the floor, finding nothing. It must have gone flying in the explosion, but why it was missing didn't matter. Without it, my only chance was to draw them in closer, so I sagged back onto the floor and lay still.

If they were properly paranoid, they'd shoot me from a distance to make sure. I relied on Shadran's ego—he'd want to gloat, to make sure we knew we'd lost. At least I hoped so, because if he didn't, this was it for us.

Even if he did, my odds weren't good. As the guards moved closer, I resigned myself to taking as many of them with me as possible, giving Mercy more time to escape.

"Still alive, Vardok?" Shadran's voice was smug and angry at the same time. "Good. You'll pay for this, this slaughter. And so will the human female when we find her."

The ground trembled, shaking under the weight of the train finally leaving the station. Was Mercy aboard? She had to be. I refused to believe otherwise. I might not have made it to freedom, but Mercy had escaped and that mattered more to me.

I grinned. I couldn't help it. "You won't find her. She's well away from here by now, out of your reach."

A stunned silence followed that statement, broken only by the distant clatter of the train picking up speed on its way toward the Hub. I wished I was aboard, not for my sake but for Mercy's. Braving the Hub on her own, she'd be in constant danger, but I had to trust that she'd be able to handle it herself.

"What have you done?" Three voices shouted in unison, the Akkarks joining Shadran in sheer horror. I laughed long and loud as they stared at me. Eventually, I forced my mirth down and replied.

"You don't understand, do you? You can't imagine someone acting unselfishly, doing something without expecting a reward. And that, gentlemen, is why you'll never know true joy."

"I will kill you for this," Shadran hissed. "Slowly."

"And I'll die happy knowing I got my mate out of your clutches."

His roar shook the room, and I smiled. Ruining Shadran's day was a pleasant bonus, and as last sights went, seeing my enemy in distress would do.

The guards' fingers tightened on their triggers, and I tensed, ready to make a final doomed attack. Death came for me, and if he took me today, he'd take my enemies too.

Outside, I heard a scream.

11

MERCY

By the time we left, there were guards in the courtyard. We moved fast and quiet, skirting the wall and sticking to the shadows where possible. Not that we needed to be stealthy—after the explosion, all the guards focused their attention on the citadel. I refused to take any chances, though. Getting caught wouldn't help Vardok if he was still alive in there.

Somehow, he held out. I was sure of that for two reasons: first, because of the guards' laser-focus on the gaping hole in the citadel wall; second, because he *had* to. I couldn't accept a universe without him in it.

I put those thoughts aside as we reached our destination, a heavy door barred from the outside.

Railhead's slave quarters stank of desperation and fear even through the sealed door, and it only got worse as we shoved the bar aside and heaved the door open. Now that we'd reached our destination, speed mattered more than stealth.

Inside was worse than I could have imagined. With no windows or ventilation, a miasma of foul air greeted us. Nothing else did, though dozens of eyes turned to us as we entered. The slaves lay against one another, crammed into a space I wouldn't have thought could hold so many, and they watched with dread as we entered.

And these are the lucky slaves, I thought, swallowing bile. *The mines are worse.*

"Don't worry, we're friends," I said. More of the huddled mass stirred, more eyes opened, but no one answered. "We're here to free you."

That got more attention, but the hope that flared in a few of the aliens' expressions was guarded. These, I realized, were people who'd learned not to hope for anything better. They wouldn't trust words.

Actions might get a better result.

I followed the chains binding one row of prisoners together. It looped through the metal collars they wore, dozens of shapes for dozens of species of aliens, and led me to the back of the chamber, away from the scant light at the doorway. Soon I was moving blind, following the chain and apologizing forced my way through the huddled mass.

At the end of the row, I found the heavy iron bolt securing the chain to the wall. The Blood Talons weren't taking any chances with their sentient 'property,' and I hoped they were right to worry.

One shot from the plasma pistol melted chain and bolt alike, the searing light drawing cries all around me. For a moment, no one moved. Then, all at once, the broken ends of the chain zipped away as slaves pulled it through the links of their collars.

I had to repeat that twice to free them all. By the end, hoarse whispers went through the group with the occasional hushed cry of joy. Whispers about revenge and freedom and escape.

"Listen to me," I said over the *plink-plink* sound of cooling metal. "You're free, and I won't tell you what to do with that freedom. But here's what I'm doing— rescuing my man and getting as many of the Blood Talons as I can while I do it. Anyone who wants revenge is free to join."

For a moment, silence reigned, and I thought I'd fucked up somehow. Then a few small cheers rose from the crowd, followed by more, stronger cries building into a tumult that I knew the guards outside would notice.

We ditched Plan Stealth a while back. Time for Plan Obvious.

"Let's go get them," I shouted. That was all it took to unleash the crowd's rage. The quiet broke in a rush of hoarse battle cries, and I found myself carried by the flood of former slaves bearing down on their hated overseers.

The aliens at the main building turned at the sound, gaping in surprised terror. Perhaps they'd imagined this day would come, but that hadn't prepared them for the reality—all their captives free, angry, and nearly on them.

Shock kept them frozen for a long moment, and then one brought up his blaster. Instinct took over, and I pulled the trigger to unleash a blast of white-hot light. By the time I'd blinked my eyes clear again, the mob rolled over where my target had stood, and I saw no trace of him.

Another crack of plasma fire sounded, and I wheeled toward it. Too slow—the mob had the shooter, pulling the blue-skinned guard down to the ground and tearing him limb from limb. I lost sight of him, which was probably for the best. The sounds he made were bad enough even without the visuals.

The guards broke under the onslaught, turning and running, only to be brought down by the people they'd abused for so long. But this was only the outer ring. Shadran and his closest guards were nowhere to be seen, and if they rallied, their firepower might still win the day. We had numbers, but no control over them. A disciplined and well-armed force, even one much smaller, would tear us apart.

I had to find them before they pulled themselves together.

It was a complete coincidence that Vardok would probably be there too. Yep. Not a factor in my decision making. I kept telling myself that as I pushed my way through the riot toward the heat-blackened hole in the citadel wall.

A guard stuck his eyeballs out, long stalks letting him keep his head safely out of view. I snapped off a shot which went wide, but at least the blinding white light would throw his own aim off.

The blast that followed tore through the air beside me, hot enough to burn. I tumbled into cover behind a concrete block, blinking back tears and trying to steady my nerves.

In my defense, no one taught me to use a plasma gun, so I had no way of knowing how bad an idea that was. Against projectile weapons, the concrete would provide decent cover. Plasma? That was another story entirely.

Eyes' shot tore into the concrete, superheating it. Unable to take the sudden change in temperature, it shattered, sending razor-sharp shards flying, only missing me by luck.

The next shot wouldn't miss. There just wasn't enough of the concrete left. If I waited there, the next explosion would cut me to shreds. Rather than wait for that, I rolled into the new gap and snapped off a shot.

Missed by a mile. Of course. This wasn't an action movie, I wasn't a great shot, and I'd apparently used up my luck. My foe's blaster pointed straight at me, and in a moment of devastating clarity, I saw his cruel smile. Finger tightening on the trigger, he took aim, and I swear I saw the blue plasma-fire ignite in the barrel of his gun.

A wall of white fur hit him, sending the shot wide and tearing the gun from his hands. My heart beat again, my own plasma gun dropping from numb fingers as I drew in a shuddering breath.

Shadran and Vardok rolled over and over, clawing at each other as they went. Red blood streaked Shadran's white fur, and I hoped that was his, not Vardok's.

The two made it to their feet and a strange silence spread around the courtyard as all the aliens turned to watch. By unspoken agreement, a truce formed, no one wanting to interrupt the duel.

Shadran paced like a tiger, all attention focused on his foe. Vardok waited, not moving from the spot, turning to keep his foe in view but otherwise motionless. It felt like that went on for *years* before Shadran's patience wore thin and he leaped at Vardok without warning.

All four arms extended to attack from different directions, he slashed at my alien mate. Who simply wasn't there.

Where Shadran moved like a wild beast, Vardok was all control and grace, like a dancer. I gasped, watching as he slipped out of danger, making it look easy, then moved past Shadran. I didn't even see the strike, but it didn't surprise me to see fresh blood welling from under that white fur.

Sharon whirled, arms striking out hard and fast, but Vardok was faster. Stepping back, he let Shadran's claws pass a fraction of an inch from his face before darting back in. His fist was a blue and gold blur, coming up into Shadran's side with a sickening crack, and then Vardok slid out of the way of Shadran's counter, striking again before he withdrew.

The white-furred bastard turned to face him, breathing in short, ragged gasps and clutching his side with one arm. That still left him with three to fight with, but everyone watching knew the duel was over. Shadran had trouble protecting himself with four arms. Reduced to three, Vardok would take him apart with ease.

Shadran knew that as well as anyone else and gave up on all pretense of honor. Instead of facing up to my alien mate or surrendering, he turned and leaped away from Vardok.

For a moment, I thought he'd decided to flee, but I wasn't that lucky. He came straight for me, and only when he was nearly on me did I realize the danger I was in. By then, it was too late. Two arms wrapped around me, taut muscle under the shaggy white fur. A third came up under my chin, claws pressing against my throat.

"Surrender now, or she dies." Shadran's breath came in shallow gasps, and I heard the effort talking cost him. One hand still pressed to his side, and the one gripping my throat trembled. That didn't make him any less dangerous, and his hands still gripped tight enough to bruise.

Vardok growled, baring his teeth and glaring at Shadran. If he'd aimed that at me, I'd have died of fear on the spot, and by rights Shadran ought to have burst into flames at the very least. I'll give him this, though. He was brave enough to weather the deadly threat.

Brave, stupid, or desperate? I didn't know, and it didn't really matter. He'd committed to this course of action, and that was that.

"Tell him to surrender and I'll spare you," he hissed into my ear. "He's too angry to reason with, but he'll listen to you, human. And you want to live."

The fight went on around us, but everything faded to shadow. The three of us became my entire universe, my life held between these two alien warriors. Would Vardok surrender if I asked him to? Maybe, but what would the Blood Talons do to him then?

Saving myself only to doom him was no victory at all.

Shadran shook me by the throat, an entirely unnecessary reminder of the danger I was in. Vardok bared his teeth but came no closer, glaring as his hands flexed and claws slid out.

He didn't trust Shadran to keep his promises, but he would take even the flimsiest of chances to protect me. I didn't trust Shadran any more than he did., but I'd take any risk to keep Vardok alive and out of the Blood Talons' clutches.

Our eyes met, and I don't know if the mate bond allowed us to feel each other's thoughts or if that was just a stress-induced hallucination. It felt like I knew him as well as I did myself, as though there were no barriers between us. And I knew what I had to do.

When I moved, it was as though we'd practiced together for years. I slid my foot forward, toes hooking under my fallen plasma gun, and kicked hard as I slammed my elbow into Shadran's injured side with all the strength I had.

The gun flew up and Vardok snatched it out of the air. Shadran's grip loosened, not enough to escape, but enough to let me duck. Claws stabbed into my neck, ready to tear out my throat.

And let go as a crack like thunder split the air. A wave of heat washed over me, the acrid scent of burning hair all I could smell. I looked back in time to see Shadran topple backward, his fur burning around the hole blasted clean through his chest. Hitting the ground with an echoing thump, he lay still. Dead.

"Don't do that again," Vardok growled. "I nearly shot you."

"But you didn't." A huge grin spread across my face as I spoke. "I knew you wouldn't."

It was easy to sound confident now that the danger had passed, and my heart felt light as a cloud. Around us, the fighting ebbed as Shadran's guards saw their leader in the dirt. Their will to fight drained, some of them surrendered, while others fled for the compound gates. Former slaves cheered and embraced, secured the surrendered guards, or hurried to find food and drink.

We'd won.

I scarcely believed it, but we'd won.

12

VARDOK

Mercy leaped into my arms as the guards melted away, and I forgot my anger at the risk she'd just taken. All around, the enemy was in flight and our allies shouted their joy to the heavens. Their mood was infectious, and I lifted my human high, spinning around and kissing her.

"Never take chances like that again," I said when our lips parted so that she could breathe. "I'd rather die than lose you."

She flushed, bit her lip, but didn't give in. "Well, I don't want to lose you, either, so you'll have to get used to me taking risks on your behalf."

I growled, hiding my amusement and respect

behind mock anger at her defiance. My human mate's blush deepened, and a tremor ran through her as she held me tight.

Then it was my turn to gasp and shiver as Mercy slid one hand down my body and into my pants. A muffled giggle at my reaction didn't help me keep my cool.

"Stop that," I said, as firmly as I could. Mercy's giggles stopped, but her insistent hand grasped my hardening cock.

"Are you *sure* you want me to stop?" Her voice, husky and low, inflamed my passions as much as her grip on me.

Reactions like this were common after battle, and this had been my Mercy's first. Having escaped death, she wanted to prove she was alive. I ought to have argued, perhaps, but how could I argue with her?

"You're treading on dangerous ground, little one. Provoke me now and I will not be able to control myself."

Another tremor ran through her, but she didn't reply. Nor did she stop caressing me, and with the energy of the fight still rushing through my veins, I felt my control slipping. I took a deep breath to calm myself, which was a mistake. Acrid smoke and the smell of blood couldn't hide my mate's scent, and I only just stopped myself from throwing Mercy to the ground and claiming her for all to see.

Turning back to the hole in the citadel's wall, I carried her inside, dashing for the stairs. She giggled in my arms, a husky, needy sound entering her voice as she clung to me, and by whatever gods there are, that sound drove me wild.

I didn't return to Heras' room. As urgent as our need for each other was, I didn't intend to bed Mercy with corpses littering the floor. Instead, I carried her to the top of the citadel, taking the stairs three at a time in my rush. The heavy door at the top barred our way for a fraction of a second—one swift kick shattered the lock and let us into Shadran's chambers.

If I'd taken the time to think about it, the luxuries would have appalled me. Thick, rich carpets, a glorious holoportrait of some Imperial noble-woman, perfumed air—the leftover luxuries of the Empire's withdrawal, hoarded by a man who aspired to be like his oppressors. I had more pressing matters to concern myself with, though, like strip-ping a wriggling human without putting her down. I stumbled through into the bathroom, leaving a trail of torn clothes as I lost patience with the unfamiliar fastenings.

The bathroom was as decadent as the rest of the suite, large enough for a dozen or more to bathe together. There was even a padded bench, almost large enough to be a bed, fixed to the far wall. Water came on automatically when we entered, blasting us from all directions. It was hot, blissfully hot, washing residue of battle from us. Sweet-smelling gel mixed with the water, and I took great joy in massaging it into Mercy's body. She grinned, returning the favor, and I shivered with delighted anticipation at her touch.

That put the smile back on her face, along with a pleasing blush. The golden glow of my enhancements sparkled off the water running down my mate, and I wondered again at my luck. How could I possibly deserve such a beauty?

Now wasn't the time for those thoughts. We'd both just lived through a battle. Both our bodies craved the comfort of the other's touch. I had never felt such desire.

Mercy gave me no time to admire her naked form before she jumped at me, tackling me with all her strength. I laughed, catching her and spinning her around, my hearts leaping as her laughter joined mine.

"My fierce warrior," I said, kissing her and pressing her against the wall, trapped between me and the warm tiles. I scraped her neck with my fangs, felt her shudder, and slid a hand down her side. Her skin was so soft, so smooth, I could have lost myself in the feel of it if she hadn't run her fingers down my enhancement marks, making me shudder again.

"You really like that, don't you?" she asked, looking me in the eye as she traced her way lower. I growled my response, hand cupping her firm ass and lifting her to me. Her lips parted under mine and our tongues met, dancing together, hers yielding to my firm pressure and her breath coming faster and faster.

When at last I broke the kiss, her pulse raced and her voice came out low, husky, unsteady. "No fair. Cheating."

"There is no rule I won't break for you, beloved."

I punctuated my statement by biting her lip, not hard enough to hurt, but enough to make her moan. Her legs trembled as she melted against me, and without my support, I thought she'd have fallen then.

No matter. She didn't have to stand. Bearing her

weight, I turned and carried her to the back of the shower chamber to lay her down on the bench that waited there. Firm but soft, it cushioned my Mercy, and I kissed my way down her body once more. I took my time, admiring the way the hot water ran across her skin, the way her blush had spread down to her breasts, the way her muscles trembled as I kissed and licked and nipped at her.

She fumbled a hand at me, trying to pull me back up for another kiss. Instead, I took her hand and kissed her fingers, her palm, her wrist. Each got a new noise from her, and each made me harden more.

The pulse of her single heartbeat raced when I pressed my lips to her wrist, and I could barely contain my need for her. But I would not rush this, nor her, and if she was to enjoy me, Mercy needed preparation.

So I pressed her down onto the soft surface, moving my lips from her hand to her breasts, feeling her nipples harden under my kisses. Tongue darting out, I licked one, then the other, and Mercy arched her back to press them to my mouth.

The noises she made had ceased to be language a while ago, but when my fingers slid between her legs, teasing with as soft a touch as I could, she let loose a cry of such passionate desire that it didn't need words to carry its meaning. Parting her legs, she arched and pressed herself to my fingers, writhing under me.

Slowly, deliberately, I pressed harder, tracing circles around her as she panted and moaned. I enjoyed every second of her rising pleasure, teasing and guiding her up to a climax that shook the room.

Her eyes sparkled as she focused on mine, her lips forming a word without sound. I understood what she was asking for well enough, and it was what I wanted, *needed*, too. Slipping between her legs, I watched her reaction as I pressed the head of my cock to her entrance and paused. Just long enough to see the need and anticipation on her face.

My first thrust buried me deep inside her, filling her, and her muscles squeezed hard. Both of us lost all control then, and in a frenzy of mating we slipped from the bench onto the floor, water battering us as Mercy gripped me and urged me onward. Again and again, her body tightened its grip on me as each climax overwhelmed her.

Each time they came closer to overwhelming me, but I held back. Restrained myself until all my willpower was spent. And when at last I could hold off my orgasm no longer, I drove her to one last climax, coming with her in a glorious wave of pleasure that swept us both into unconsciousness in each other's arms.

MERCY

At some point, the water stopped. I wasn't sure when it happened, too wrapped up in the exhausted joy of curling up against my alien warrior and listening to his twin heartbeats.

Vardok's hand played gently with my hair, a wonderfully calming sensation. I could have stayed there forever and would have, given half a chance. Warm air blew from the walls, drying us as we snuggled, and the floor was surprisingly comfortable. I didn't have much good to say about the aliens who'd captured and tried to enslave me, but I had to admit they made excellent bathrooms.

Unfortunately, Vardok didn't let me rest for long. He shifted restlessly, then sat up, taking me with him.

"Nooo, just a few more minutes," I said, twisting to look up at him. His fond smile lit up the room. "Or hours. A few more hours and I'll move."

That got a laugh from him, booming and echoing in the small space. Under it, though, I saw a melancholy. Something was wrong.

I groaned and pulled myself up with Vardok's help. My muscles were still weak, shaking from the activities of the night. Both the fun and the terrifying parts had left a mark on me.

"Okay, big guy, what's up?"

His lips twisted. "I should know better than to keep things from you, but I didn't want to spoil our last night together."

Forget leading a slave revolt. Those were words to freeze my heart. I looked up at him, unbelieving and unable to find words.

"What? How? What?" Not exactly piercing questions, but they were what came out when I tried to speak.

Vardok carefully brushed the damp hair from my face, running his fingers down my cheek. "Tomorrow, another train will arrive. We'll take it to the Hub and find a ship to take you home. I will make certain you are safe, but I cannot leave with you."

Warmth was a distant memory. My heart froze,

my blood was ice, and I sat bolt upright, staring at Vardok. "I thought this mate bond thing was for life?"

"It is." His words came out heavy, dulled by pain, and that only made it worse. He suffered, I suffered, and for what? "We are bound together, but that doesn't erase my responsibilities here. I owe these people a debt for the years I worked for the Blood Talons, and now that I am free, I must repay it. The bulk of the gang is at the mines, and they need Railhead—they'll try to retake it, they have no choice."

Of course he was staying for a noble reason, the bastard. I couldn't even argue with that. While I sailed back to my life on Earth, he'd be here, protecting the weak...

Fuck it. I knew what I had to do.

"You're right, these people need your help," I said. Vardok started to speak, but I kept going. I had to, before I lost my nerve. "They need *our* help. I'm not going anywhere without you."

Vardok blinked, mouth opening to speak, closing again without a word. He ran a hand through his wet hair, droplets running down his chest and distracting me until I dragged my gaze back up to his.

"You can't," he managed finally. "It is too dangerous, and I won't have you hurt."

"Then you have to let me stay." I crossed my arms and furrowed my brow. "Here, you can protect me. If I'm on Earth, I'm out of your hands. You'll never know if I'm still alive."

Silence stretched between us, both of us lost for words. Eventually, I spoke again.

"Neither of us wants us to separate, right? If you're here, so am I, and the rest is details. We can work them out *later*. And there's something else—I wasn't the only abducted human aboard that slaver ship, whatever happened to it. I don't know if any of the other stasis pods crashed here, but if they did, perhaps we can find and help them?"

Vardok growled and shook his head, but it wasn't a refusal. "If you stay here, your life will probably be short and, unless we find more humans who fell from the sky, you'll not see another of your kind again. I cannot ask that of you."

"Then don't," I told him, snuggling back into him and kissing his bare skin. "You're not asking. I'm telling you I *want* to stay with you. You don't get to make every decision for me, you know."

As fun as that sounds, I didn't add. No reason to encourage him; not now.

Strong alien arms pulled me close, held me tight, and I looked up at Vardok. Golden light shone from the bands around his body, and he had the smile of someone who couldn't quite believe his luck.

That was fair. I couldn't believe mine, either. Fortunately, we'd have the rest of our lives to get used to the idea.

EPILOGUE

A year later, I stood on the wall of Railhead watching the train approach across the water. The rails it rode on were low enough that the train kicked up a spray; even a mild storm could cut us off from the mainland.

That was okay, though. We survived just fine. Fighting the remaining Blood Talons had been tough work, but once Vardok got rid of them, there were plenty of resources on the island for everyone. All it took was being willing to share.

A heavy hand landed on my shoulder, and I managed not to jump out of my skin. "Darling, beloved, love of my life. You have *got to* stop sneaking up on me like that."

"Sorry," he said, amusement giving the lie to his word. A kiss on my neck made a better apology, and I leaned back into his chest with a soft moan.

A year in and I'd still not gotten the hang of staying annoyed with him, no matter how much he aggravated me. The thought made me chuckle, which became a gasp as his kiss turned into a bite, setting off fireworks in my nervous system.

"No fair," I whispered. "Especially when I can't jump you."

"You will just have to save it up for when we have enough privacy."

My cheeks warmed, and I hid a smile. Vardok might make fun of me for wanting privacy when we mated, but he loved using that to tease me. I bit my lower lip, trying to ignore the way his hand wandered down my back, fingertips tracing delicious patterns through my thin top.

"We have guests arriving," I pointed out.

"Let them wait."

"And we're in public."

"Let them watch."

"And you are impossible."

Vardok laughed. "Yes. I am. Mercy, my sweet mate, you drive me wild with need. I will take you every chance I have, you know this."

My blush deepened, and I turned to face him. This was the topic we needed to discuss. "Not that I don't want you to, love, but I might need a break. I'm…"

Coward that I am, I trailed off there. Vardok didn't push, holding me against him and giving me time to work out my words as we watched the train zoom closer. It had nearly reached the shore by the time he broke the silence.

"Is there a problem?" His voice was full of concern. A master warrior who could kill dozens without flinching, and now he sounded almost frightened. It was ridiculous, but true.

"I… I'm…" I trailed off again.

"Is something wrong with the baby?"

I started, pulling away and whirling to face him. "What? No! But how—"

I cut off, stopping myself from babbling, and counted to three before starting over.

"How did you know? I've been agonizing about telling you all morning."

Perrix, the closest thing we had to a doctor at Railhead, had confirmed it this morning. If he'd gone behind my back to tell Vardok, I'd…

*You'll keep on being friendly with him, idiot. What part of **'closest thing to a doctor'** don't you get? You need* *him.* My subconscious wasn't in a mood to put up with my melodrama, and it wasn't wrong.

Vardok frowned. "How could I not know? Your scent has changed, your taste, everything."

"And you didn't say anything?"

"I wanted to respect your custom, and you didn't mention it. So I waited. It wasn't easy to hide my joy at the news, but your comfort came first."

My cheeks burned. "And you're okay with it?"

"No," he intoned. "I am overjoyed, my love, that you carry our child. I can't wait to meet them and help raise them. Though if they take after you, my love, it will take both of us to keep her out of trouble."

"Hey," I protested with a grin, and he chuckled. I let my eyes drift shut as my alien lover's arms folded around me and a weight lifted from my soul. He might be impossible, but he was mine, and we'd meet any challenges the future brought. Together.

The End

Thank you for reading *Alien's Mercy!* Please take a moment to leave an opinion about the book, I appreciate every review.

And remember to check out the rest of the Outlaw Planet Mates series!

An exciting new multi-author series of standalone books by some of the most exciting authors in science fiction romance!

ALIEN'S MERCY, by Leslie Chase (that's this book!)

ALIEN'S TREASURE, by Elin Wyn (Out on November 10th)

ALIEN'S CHALLENGE, by Nancey Cummings (Out on November 12th)

ALIEN'S STONE HEART, by Lynnea Lee (Out on November 14th)

ALIEN'S FATE, by Eden Ember (Out on November 15th)

ALIENS' SACRIFICE, by Cady Austin (Out on November 16th)

ALIEN'S JEWEL, by Ava York (Out on November 17th)

ALIEN'S SURRENDER, by Harper Rosling (Out on November 18th)

LESLIE CHASE

I love writing, and especially enjoy writing sexy science fiction and paranormal romances. It lets my imagination run free and my ideas come to life! When I'm not writing, I'm busy thinking about what to write next or researching it – yes, damn it, looking at castles and swords and spaceships counts as research.

If you enjoy my books, please let me know with a review. Reviews are really important and I appreciate every one. If you'd like to be kept up to date on my new releases, you can sign up for my email newsletter by **following this link** — subscribers get a free science fiction romance novella!

www.leslie-chase.com

facebook.com/lesliechaseauthor

twitter.com/lchasewrites

bookbub.com/authors/leslie-chase

amazon.com/Leslie-Chase/e/B019S4QW3C

CRASHLAND COLONY ROMANCES

AURIC

Crashed on an unexplored planet, with only an alien warrior and a holographic cat for company... what's a girl to do?

TORRAN

Stranded on the wrong planet, captured by brutal alien raiders, the only good thing about Lisa's situation is Torran. He's a dangerous alien warrior - who also happens to be the hottest man she's ever met. Strong, protective, and lethal, he's everything she could want or need.

Perhaps she shouldn't have shot him on sight?

RONAN

Trapped with a sexy alien warrior, a holographic owl, and a mystery she needs to solve. Becca doesn't like the prytheen, she doesn't trust them, and she is absolutely not interested in this one.

So why is she having so much trouble keeping her hands off him?

CRASHLAND CASTAWAY ROMANCES

Bound to the Alien Barbarian

Crashed on the wrong planet.

Stuck with the wrong man.

Taken by the right alien.

Waking up to find she's one of only two humans to survive a crash is bad. Being captured by an alien warrior who isn't sure if she's a demon is worse. But when the alien claims her as his mate, she doesn't know if she wants to escape…

Chained to the Alien Champion

Marakz is the hottest man I've ever seen. Also the most infuriating. At least Lord Pouncington likes him…

Diplomatic contact between the Joint Colony and the Zrin gets off to a rocky start when the Sri champion sees his mate amongst the humans. When disaster strikes, she's his first thought — but is he rescuing her or capturing her?

Megan isn't sure she cares.

questions. She should be insufferable, but instead he finds himself unable to get the sassy woman out of his mind…

MATED TO THE ALIEN LORD

a Celestial Mates novel by Leslie Chase

Love is never easy. Love on an alien world is downright dangerous!

With her life on Earth going nowhere, Gemma needs a fresh start. Enter the Celestial Mates Agency, who say they can match her with the perfect alien. And despite the dangers of his planet, Corvax is everything she could have asked for — impossibly hot, brave, and huge.

Now that she's seen him, there's no way she's going back.

ARCANE AFFAIRS AGENCY

A shared world of shifters, vampires, far, and witches - full of everything that goes bump in the night! Check out the full list of books **here**.

THE BEAR AND THE HEIR, by Leslie Chase

When Cole North arrives in Argent Falls to investigate reports of magical storms, he doesn't expect much to come of it. Not after the series of pointless missions the Arcane Affairs Agency has sent him on recently. This time, though, it's different. The small town is plagued by bizarre weather, the storms are trying to warn him off, and there are *fae* running wild. And then there's Fiona.

No matter how much the bear shifter tries to focus on his mission, he can't get the hot, curvy girl out of his head. But the fae are after her too – and when they try and kidnap her, Cole's mission and his feelings for Fiona collide.

GUARDIAN BEARS

Ex-military bear shifters providing protection from the threats no one else can deal with. Each book is a stand-alone plot, as the sexy bears find their curvy mates.

1. **GUARDIAN BEARS: MARCUS**
2. **GUARDIAN BEARS: LUCAS**
3. **GUARDIAN BEARS: KARL**

TIGER'S SWORD

A four-part paranormal romance serial about Maxwell Walters, billionaire tiger shifter, and his curvy mate Lenore.

Box Set, collecting all four parts

1. **Tiger's Hunt**
2. **Tiger's Den**
3. **Tiger's Claws**
4. **Tiger's Heart**